Praise for Bret Easton Ellis's

Imperial Bedrooms

"This sequel is very much on target. . . . [Ellis] uses the thriller framework to infuse nerve-rending unease into this look at Tinseltown mores. Grade: A–."
>—*Entertainment Weekly*

"Taut and ultimately terrifying. . . . In six novels, the author has emerged as one of the most gifted and serious novelists working in America today." —*Financial Times*

"Enough talk of [Ellis's] literary genius, let's call him what he really is: a terrific horror writer. . . . An absolute creepfest [and] a festival of panting paranoia."
>—*Chicago Sun-Times*

"Brutally conceived, and effectively done....There is no doubt that Ellis retains the ability to startle and disquiet."
>—*The Times Literary Supplement* (London)

"Arrestingly spare. . . . *Imperial Bedrooms* will leave you feeling bruised, guarded and a little nervous about noises at night. . . . What you really notice is Ellis's newfound love of noir. He's reinvigorated and ready to get mysterious and mean. . . . As ever, Ellis's details crystallize into elegant remoteness (and) if this is shallowness, the word needs a new definition." —*Time Out New York*

Bret Easton Ellis

Imperial Bedrooms

Bret Easton Ellis is also the author of *American Psycho*, *Glamorama*, *The Informers*, *Less Than Zero*, *Lunar Park*, and *The Rules of Attraction*. His work has been translated into twenty-seven languages. He lives in Los Angeles.

www.castonellis.com

Imperial Bedrooms

Bret Easton Ellis

Imperial Bedrooms

Vintage Contemporaries
Vintage Books
A Division of Random House, Inc.
New York

FIRST VINTAGE CONTEMPORARIES EDITION, MAY 2011

The Library of Congress has cataloged the Knopf edition as follows:
Ellis, Bret Easton.
Imperial bedrooms / by Bret Easton Ellis.—1st ed.
1. Middle-aged men—Fiction. 2. Male friendship—Fiction.
3. Generation X—Fiction. 4. City and town life—California—
Los Angeles—Fiction. 5. Los Angeles (Calif.)—Fiction. I. Title.
PS3555.L5937153   2010
813'54—dc22   2009041690

Vintage ISBN: 978-0-307-27869-2

www.vintagebooks.com

Printed in the United States of America
10   9   8   7   6

FOR R.T.

History repeats the old conceits,
the glib replies, the same defeats . . .

ELVIS COSTELLO, "Beyond Belief"

There is no trap so deadly as the trap
you set for yourself.

RAYMOND CHANDLER, *The Long Goodbye*

Imperial Bedrooms

They had made a movie about us. The movie was based on a book written by someone we knew. The book was a simple thing about four weeks in the city we grew up in and for the most part was an accurate portrayal. It was labeled fiction but only a few details had been altered and our names weren't changed and there was nothing in it that hadn't happened. For example, there actually had been a screening of a snuff film in that bedroom in Malibu on a January afternoon, and yes, I had walked out onto the deck overlooking the Pacific where the author tried to console me, assuring me that the screams of the children being tortured were faked, but he was smiling as he said this and I had to turn away. Other examples: my girlfriend had in fact run over a coyote in the canyons below Mulholland, and a Christmas Eve dinner at Chasen's with my family that I had casually complained about to the author was faithfully rendered. And a twelve-year-old girl really had been gang-raped—I was in that room in West Hollywood with the writer, who in the book noted just a vague reluctance on my part and failed to accurately describe how I had actually felt that night— the desire, the shock, how afraid I was of the writer, a blond and isolated boy whom the girl I was dating had halfway fallen in love with. But the writer would never fully return her love because he was too lost in his own passivity to make the connection she needed from him, and so she had turned to me, but by then it was too late, and because the writer resented that she had turned to me I became the handsome and dazed narrator, incapable of love or kindness. That's how I became the damaged party boy who wandered through the wreckage, blood streaming from his nose, asking questions that never required answers. That's how I became the boy who never understood how anything worked. That's how I became the boy who wouldn't save a friend. That's how I became the boy who couldn't love the girl.

The scenes from the novel that hurt the most chronicled my relationship with Blair, especially in a scene near the novel's end when I broke it off with her on a restaurant patio overlooking Sunset Boulevard and where a billboard that read DISAPPEAR HERE kept distracting me (the author added that I was wearing sunglasses when I told Blair that I never loved her). I hadn't mentioned that painful afternoon to the author but it appeared verbatim in the book and that's when I stopped talking to Blair and couldn't listen to the Elvis Costello songs we knew by heart ("You Little Fool," "Man Out of Time," "Watch Your Step") and yes, she had given me a scarf at a Christmas party, and yes, she had danced over to me mouthing Culture Club's "Do You Really Want to Hurt Me?" and yes, she had called me "a fox," and yes, she found out I had slept with a girl I picked up on a rainy night at the Whisky, and yes, the author had informed her of that. He wasn't, I realized when I read those scenes concerning Blair and myself, close to any of us—except of course to Blair, and really not even to her. He was simply someone who floated through our lives and didn't seem to care how flatly he perceived everyone or that he'd shared our secret failures with the world, showcasing the youthful indifference, the gleaming nihilism, glamorizing the horror of it all.

But there was no point in being angry with him. When the book was published in the spring of 1985, the author had already left Los Angeles. In 1982 he attended the same small college in New Hampshire that I'd tried to disappear into, and where we had little or no contact. (There's a chapter in his second novel, which takes place at Camden, where he parodies Clay—just another gesture, another cruel reminder of how he felt about me. Careless and not particularly biting, it was easier to shrug off than anything in the first book which depicted me as an inarticulate zombie confused by the irony of Randy Newman's "I Love L.A.") Because of his presence I stayed at Camden only one year and then transferred to Brown in 1983 though in the second novel I'm still in New Hampshire during the fall term of 1985. I told myself it shouldn't bother me, but the success of the first book hovered within my sight lines for an uncomfortably long time. This partly had to do with my wanting to become a writer as well, and that I had wanted to write that first novel the author had written after I finished reading it—it was my life and he had hijacked it. But I quickly had to accept that I didn't have the talent or the drive. I didn't have the patience. I just wanted to be able to do it. I made a few lame, slashing attempts and realized after graduating from Brown in 1986 that it was never going to happen.

The only person who expressed any embarrassment or disdain about the novel was Julian Wells—Blair was still in love with the author and didn't care, nor did much of the supporting cast—but Julian did so in a gleefully arrogant manner that verged on excitement, even though the author had exposed not only Julian's heroin addiction but also the fact that he was basically a hustler in debt to a drug dealer (Finn Delaney) and pimped out to men visiting from Manhattan or Chicago or San Francisco in the hotels that lined Sunset from Beverly Hills to Silver Lake. Julian, wasted and self-pitying, had told the author everything, and there was something about the book being widely read and costarring Julian that seemed to give Julian some kind of focus that bordered on hope and I think he was secretly pleased with it because Julian had no shame—he only pretended that he did. And Julian was even more excited when the movie version opened in the fall of 1987, just two years after the novel was published.

I remember my trepidation about the movie began on a warm October night three weeks prior to its theatrical release, in a screening room on the 20th Century Fox lot. I was sitting between Trent Burroughs and Julian, who wasn't clean yet and kept biting his nails, squirming in the plush black chair with anticipation. (I saw Blair walk in with

Alana and Kim and trailing Rip Millar. I ignored her.) The movie was very different from the book in that there was nothing from the book in the movie. Despite everything—all the pain I felt, the betrayal—I couldn't help but recognize a truth while sitting in that screening room. In the book everything about me had happened. The book was something I simply couldn't disavow. The book was blunt and had an honesty about it, whereas the movie was just a beautiful lie. (It was also a bummer: very colorful and busy but also grim and expensive, and it didn't recoup its cost when released that November.) In the movie I was played by an actor who actually looked more like me than the character the author portrayed in the book: I wasn't blond, I wasn't tan, and neither was the actor. I also suddenly became the movie's moral compass, spouting AA jargon, castigating everyone's drug use and trying to save Julian. ("I'll sell my car," I warn the actor playing Julian's dealer. "Whatever it takes.") This was slightly less true of the adaptation of Blair's character, played by a girl who actually seemed like she belonged in our group—jittery, sexually available, easily wounded. Julian became the sentimentalized version of himself, acted by a talented, sad-faced clown, who has an affair with Blair and then realizes he has to let her go because I was his best bud. "Be good to her," Julian tells Clay. "She really deserves it." The sheer hypocrisy of this scene must have made the author blanch. Smiling secretly to myself with perverse satisfaction when the actor delivered that line, I then glanced at Blair in the darkness of the screening room.

As the movie glided across the giant screen, restlessness began to reverberate in the hushed auditorium. The audience—the book's actual cast—quickly realized what had happened. The reason the movie dropped everything that made the novel real was because there was no way the parents who ran the studio would ever expose their children in the same black light the book did. The movie was begging for our sympathy whereas the book didn't give a shit. And attitudes about drugs and sex had shifted quickly from 1985 to 1987 (and a regime change at the studio didn't help) so the source material—surprisingly conservative despite its surface immorality—had to be reshaped. The best way to look at the movie was as modern eighties noir—the cinematography was breathtaking—and I sighed as it kept streaming forward, interested in only a few things: the new and gentle details of my parents mildly amused me, as did Blair finding her divorced father with his girlfriend on Christmas Eve instead of with a boy named Jared (Blair's father died of AIDS in 1992 while still married to Blair's mother). But the thing I remember most about that screening in October twenty years ago was the moment Julian grasped my hand that had gone numb on the armrest separating our seats. He did this because in the book Julian Wells lived but in the movie's new scenario he had to die. He had to be punished for all of his sins. That's what the movie demanded. (Later, as a screenwriter, I learned it's what all movies demanded.) When this scene occurred, in the last ten minutes, Julian looked at me in the darkness, stunned. "I died," he whispered. "They killed me off." I waited a beat before sighing, "But you're still here." Julian turned back to the screen and soon the movie ended, the credits rolling over the palm trees as I (improbably) take Blair back to my college while Roy Orbison wails a song about how life fades away.

The real Julian Wells didn't die in a cherry-red convertible, overdosing on a highway in Joshua Tree while a choir soared over the sound track. The real Julian Wells was murdered over twenty years later, his body dumped behind an abandoned apartment building in Los Feliz after he had been tortured to death at another location. His head was crushed—his face struck with such force that it had partly folded in on itself—and he had been stabbed so brutally that the L.A. coroner's office counted one hundred fifty-nine wounds from three different knives, many of them overlapping. His body was discovered by a group of kids who went to CalArts and were cruising through the streets off of Hillhurst in a convertible BMW looking for a parking space. When they saw the body they thought the "thing" lying by a trash bin was—and I'm quoting the first *Los Angeles Times* article on the front page of the California section about the Julian Wells murder—"a flag." I had to stop when I hit upon that word and start reading the article again from the beginning. The students who found Julian thought this because Julian was wearing a white Tom Ford suit (it had belonged to him but it wasn't something he was wearing the night he was abducted) and their immediate reaction seemed halfway logical since the jacket and pants were streaked with red. (Julian had been stripped before he was killed and then re-dressed.) But if they thought it was a "flag" my immediate question was: then where was the blue? If the body resembled a flag, I kept wondering, then where was the blue? And then I realized: it was his head. The students thought it was a flag because Julian had lost so much blood that his crumpled face was a blue so dark it was almost black.

But then I should have realized this sooner because, in my own way, I had put Julian there, and I'd seen what had happened to him in another—and very different—movie.

The blue Jeep starts following us on the 405 somewhere between LAX and the Wilshire exit. I notice it only because the driver's eyes have been glancing into the rearview mirror above the windshield I've been gazing out of, at the lanes of red taillights streaming toward the hills, drunk, in the backseat, ominous hip-hop playing softly through the speakers, my phone glowing in my lap with texts I can't read coming in from an actress I was hitting on earlier that afternoon in the American Airlines first-class lounge at JFK (she had been reading my palm and we were both giggling), other messages from Laurie in New York a total blur. The Jeep follows the sedan across Sunset, passing the mansions draped with Christmas lights while I'm nervously chewing mints from a tin of Altoids, failing to mask my gin-soaked breath, and then the blue Jeep makes the same right and rolls toward the Doheny Plaza, tailing us as if it were a lost child. But as the sedan swerves into the driveway where the valet and a security guard look up from smoking cigarettes beneath a towering palm, the Jeep hesitates before it keeps rolling down Doheny toward Santa Monica Boulevard. The hesitation makes it clear that we were guiding it somewhere. I stumble out of the car and watch as the Jeep slowly brakes before turning onto Elevado Street. It's warm but I'm shivering in a pair of frayed sweats and a torn Nike hoodie, everything loose because of the weight I dropped that fall, the sleeves damp from a drink I spilled during the flight. It's midnight in December and I've been away for four months.

"I thought that car was following us," the driver says, opening the trunk. "It kept moving lanes with us. It tailed us all the way here."

"What do you think it wanted?" I ask.

The night doorman, whom I don't recognize, walks down the ramp leading from the lobby to the driveway to help me with my bags. I overtip the driver and he gets back into the sedan and pulls out onto Doheny to pick up his next passenger at LAX, an arrival from Dallas. The valet and the security guard nod silently as I walk past them, following the doorman into the lobby. The doorman places the bags in the elevator and says before the doors close, cutting him off, "Welcome back."

Walking down the Art Deco hallway on the fifteenth floor of the Doheny Plaza I'm aware of the faint scent of pine, and then I see a wreath has been hung on the black double doors of 1508. And inside the condo a Christmas tree sits discreetly in the corner of the living room, sparkling with white lights. A note in the kitchen from the housekeeper is a reminder of what I owe her, listing the supplies she's bought, and next to that a small stack of mail that hadn't been forwarded to the New York address. I bought the condo two years ago—leaving the El Royale after a decade of renting—from the parents of a wealthy West Hollywood party boy who had been redesigning the space when after a night of clubbing he died unexpectedly in his sleep. The designer the boy had hired finished the job, and the dead boy's parents hurriedly put it on the market. Minimally decorated in soft beiges and grays with hardwood floors and recessed lighting, it's only twelve hundred square feet—a master bedroom, an office, an immaculate living room opening into a futuristic, sterile kitchen—but the entire window wall that runs the length of the living room is actually a sliding glass door divided into five panels that I push open to air the condo out, and where the large white-tiled balcony drops into an epic view of the city that reaches from the skyscrapers downtown, the dark forests of Beverly Hills, the towers of Century City and Westwood, then all the way to Santa Monica and the edge of the Pacific. The view is impressive without becoming a study in isolation; it's more intimate than the one a friend had who lived on

Appian Way, which was so far above the city it seemed as if you were looking at a vast and abandoned world laid out in anonymous grids and quadrants, a view that confirmed you were much more alone than you thought you were, a view that inspired the flickering thoughts of suicide. The view from the Doheny Plaza is so tactile that you can almost touch the blues and greens of the design center on Melrose. Because of how high I am above the city it's a good place to hide when working in L.A. Tonight the sky is violet-tinged and there's a mist.

After pouring myself a tumbler of Grey Goose that was left in the freezer when I escaped last August, I'm about to turn on the balcony lights but then stop and move slowly out into the shadow of the overhang. The blue Jeep is parked on the corner of Elevado and Doheny. From inside the Jeep a cell phone glows. I realize the hand not holding the vodka is now clenched into a fist. The fear returns as I gaze at the Jeep. And then a flash of light: someone lit a cigarette. From behind me the phone rings. I don't answer it.

The reason I've sold myself on being back in Los Angeles: the casting of *The Listeners* is under way. The producer who had brought me in to adapt the complicated novel it was based on was so relieved when I figured it out that he had almost instantly hired an enthusiastic director, and the three of us were acting as collaborators (even after a tense negotiation where my lawyer and manager insisted that I receive a producing credit as well). They had already cast the four adult leads but their children were trickier and more specific roles and the director and the producer wanted my input. This is the official reason why I'm in L.A. But, really, coming back to the city is an excuse to escape New York and whatever had happened to me there that fall.

The cell vibrates inside my pocket. I glance at it curiously. A text from Julian, a person I haven't had any contact with in over a year. *When do you get back? Are you here? Wanna hang?* Almost automatically the landline rings. I move into the kitchen and look at the receiver. PRIVATE NAME. PRIVATE NUMBER. After four rings, whoever is calling hangs up. When I look back outside the mist keeps drifting in over the city, enveloping everything.

I go into my office without turning on the lights. I check e-mails from all of the accounts: reminder of a dinner with the Germans financing a script, another director meeting, my TV agent asking if I've finished the Sony pilot yet, a couple of young actors wanting to know what's happening with *The Listeners*, a series of invites to various Christmas parties, my trainer at Equinox—having heard from another client that I'm back—wondering if I'd like to book any sessions. I take an Ambien to get to sleep since there's not enough vodka. When I move to the bedroom window and look down at Elevado, the Jeep is pulling away, its headlights flashing, and it turns onto Doheny, then moves up toward Sunset, and in the closet I find a few things left by a girl who hung around last summer, and suddenly I don't want to think of where she might be at this moment. I get another text from Laurie: *Do you still want me?* It's almost four in the morning in the apartment below Union Square. So many people died last year: the accidental overdose, the car wreck in East Hampton, the surprise illness. People just disappeared. I fall asleep to the music coming from the Abbey, a song from the past, "Hungry Like the Wolf," rising faintly above the leaping chatter of the club, transporting me for one long moment into someone both young and old. Sadness: it's everywhere.

The premiere is at the Chinese tonight and it's a movie that has something to do with confronting evil, a situation set up so obviously that the movie becomes safely vague in a way that will entice the studio to buy awards for it, in fact there's a campaign already under way, and I'm with the director and the producer of *The Listeners* and we drift with the rest of the crowd across Hollywood Boulevard to the Roosevelt for the after-party where paparazzi cling to the hotel's entrance and I immediately grab a drink at the bar while the producer disappears into the bathroom and the director stands next to me talking on the phone to his wife, who's in Australia. When I scan the darkened room, smiling back at unfamiliar people, the fear returns and soon it's everywhere and it keeps streaming forward: it's in the looming success of the film we just watched, it's in the young actors' seductive questions about possible roles in *The Listeners,* and it's in the texts they send walking away, their faces glowing from the cell light as they cross the cavernous lobby, and it's in the spray-on tans and the teeth stained white. *I've been in New York the last four months* is the mantra, my mask an expressionless smile. Finally the producer appears from behind a Christmas tree and says, "Let's get out of here," then mentions something about a couple of parties up in the hills, and Laurie keeps texting from New York (*Hey. You.*) and I cannot get it out of my head that someone in this room is following me. Sudden rapid camera flashes are a distraction, but the pale fear returns when I realize whoever was in that blue Jeep last night is probably in the crowd.

We head west on Sunset in the producer's Porsche and then turn up Doheny to the first of two parties Mark wants to hit, the director following us in a black Jaguar, and we start speeding past the bird streets until we spot a valet. Small decorated firs surround the bar I'm standing at pretending to listen while a grinning actor tells me what he's got lined up and I'm drunkenly staring at the gorgeous girl he's with, U2 Christmas songs drowning everything out, and guys in Band of Outsiders suits sit on a low-slung ivory sofa snorting lines off a long glass cocktail table, and when someone offers me a bump I'm tempted but decline knowing where that will lead. The producer, buzzed, needs to hit another party in Bel Air, and I'm drunk enough to let him maneuver me out of this one even though there's a vague shot of getting laid here. The producer wants to meet someone at the party in Bel Air, it's business in Bel Air, his presence in Bel Air is supposed to prove something about his status, and my eyes wander over to the boys barely old enough to drive swimming in the heated pool, girls in string bikinis and high heels lounging by the Jacuzzi, anime sculptures everywhere, a mosaic of youth, a place you don't really belong anymore.

At the house in the upper reaches of Bel Air, the producer loses me and I move from room to room and become momentarily disoriented when I see Trent Burroughs and everything gets complicated while I try and sync myself with the party, and then I soberly realize that this is the house where Trent and Blair live. There's no recourse except to have another drink. That I'm not driving is the consolation. Trent is standing with a manager and two agents—all of them gay, one engaged to a woman, the other two still in the closet. I know Trent's sleeping with the junior agent, blond with fake white teeth, so blandly good-looking he's not even a variation on a type. I realize I have nothing to say to Trent Burroughs as I tell him, "I've been in New York the last four months." New Age Christmas music fails to warm up the chilly vibe. I'm suddenly unsure about everything.

Trent looks at me, nodding, slightly bewildered by my presence. He knows he needs to say something. "So, that's great about *The Listeners*. It's really happening."

"That's what they tell me."

After the nonconversation starts itself we enter into a hazy area about a supposed friend of ours, someone named Kelly.

"Kelly disappeared," Trent says, straining. "Have you heard anything?"

"Oh, yeah?" I ask, and then, "Wait, what do you mean?"

"Kelly Montrose. He disappeared. No one can find him."

Pause. "What happened?"

"He went out to Palm Springs," Trent says. "They think maybe he met someone online."

Trent seems to want a reaction. I stare back.

"That's strange," I murmur disinterestedly. "Or . . . is he prone to things like that?"

Trent looks at me as if something has been confirmed, and then reveals his disgust.

"*Prone?* No, Clay, he's not *prone* to things like that."

"Trent—"

Walking away from me, Trent says, "He's probably dead, Clay."

On the veranda overlooking the massive lit pool bordered by palms wrapped in white Christmas lights, I'm smoking a cigarette, contemplating another text from Julian.

I look up from the phone when a shadow steps slowly out of the darkness and it's such a dramatic moment—her beauty and my subsequent reaction to it—that I have to laugh, and she just stares at me, smiling, maybe buzzed, maybe wasted. This is the girl who would usually make me afraid, but tonight she doesn't. The look is blond and wholesome, mid-western, distinctly American, not what I'm usually into. She's obviously an actress because girls who look like this aren't out here for any other reason, and she just gazes at me like this is all a dare. So I make it one.

"Do you want to be in a movie?" I ask her, swaying.

The girl keeps smiling. "Why? Do you have a movie you want to put me in?"

Then the smile freezes and quickly fades as she glances behind me.

I turn around and squint at the woman heading toward us, backlit by the room she's leaving.

When I turn back around the girl's walking away, her silhouette enhanced by the glow of the pool, and from somewhere in the darkness there's the sound of a fountain splashing, and then the girl is replaced.

"Who was that?" Blair asks.

"Merry Christmas."

"Why are you here?"

"I was invited."

"No. You weren't."

"My friends brought me."

"Friends? Congratulations."

"Merry Christmas" again is all I can offer.

"Who was that girl you were talking to?"

I turn around and glance back into the darkness. "I don't know."

Blair sighs. "I thought you were in New York."

"I'm back and forth."

She just stares at me.

"Yeah." And then: "You and Trent still happy?"

"Why are you here tonight? Who are you with?"

"I didn't know this was your place," I say, looking away. "I'm sorry."

"Why don't you know these things?"

"Because you haven't talked to me in two years."

Another text from Julian tells me to meet him at the Polo Lounge. Not wanting to go back to the condo, I have the producer drop me off at the Beverly Hills Hotel. Outside, on the patio, next to a heat lamp, Julian sits in a booth, his face glowing while he texts someone. He looks up, smiles. As soon as I slide into the booth a waiter appears and I order a Belvedere on the rocks. When I offer Julian a questioning look he taps a bottle of Fiji water I hadn't noticed before and says, "I'm not drinking."

I take this in and deliberate slightly. "Because . . . you have to drive?"

"No," he says. "I've been sober for about a year."

"That's a little drastic."

Julian glances at his phone, then back at me.

"And how's that going?" I ask.

"It's hard." He shrugs.

"You more cheerful now?"

"Clay . . ."

"Can we smoke out here?"

The waiter brings the drink.

"How was the premiere?" Julian asks.

"Not a soul in sight." I sigh, studying the tumbler of vodka.

"So you're back from New York for how long?"

"I don't know yet."

He tries again. "How's *The Listeners* coming?" he asks with a sudden interest, trying to move me into the same world.

I gaze at him, then answer cautiously. "It's coming along. We're casting." I wait as long as I can, then I knock back the drink and light a cigarette. "For some reason the producer and director think my input's important. *Valuable.* They're *artists.*" I take a drag off the cigarette. "It's basically a joke."

"I think it's cool," Julian says. "It's all about control, right?" He considers something. "It's not a joke. You should take it seriously. I mean, you're also one of the producers—"

I cut him off. "Why have you been tracking this?"

"It's a big deal and—"

"Julian, it's a movie," I say. "Why have you been tracking this? It's just another movie."

"Maybe for you."

"What does that mean?"

"Maybe for others it's something else," Julian says. "Something more meaningful."

"I get where you're coming from, but there's a vampire in it."

Inside, the piano player's doing jazzy riffs on Christmas carols. I concentrate on that. I'm already locked out of everything. It's that time of night when I've entered the dead zone and I'm not coming out.

"What happened to that girl you were seeing?" he asks.

"Laurie? In New York?"

"No, out here. Last summer." He pauses. "The actress."

I try to pause but fail. "Meghan," I say casually.

"Right." He draws the word out.

"I really have no idea." I lift the glass, rattle the ice around.

Julian innocently glances at me, his eyes widening slightly. This makes it clear he has information he wants to give me. I realize that I sat here, in this very same booth, one afternoon with Blair, in a different era, something I wouldn't have remembered if I hadn't seen her tonight.

"Are we lost again, Julian?" I sigh. "Are we gonna play out another scene?"

"Hey, you've been gone a long time and—"

"How do you even know about that?" I ask suddenly. "You and I weren't hanging then."

"What do you mean?" he asks. "I saw you last summer."

"How do you know about Meghan Reynolds?"

"Someone told me you were helping her out . . . giving her a break—"

"We were fucking, Julian."

"She said that you—"

"I don't care what she said." I stand up. "Everyone lies."

"Hey," he says softly. "It's just a code."

"No. Everyone lies." I stub the cigarette out.

"It's just another language you have to learn." Then he delicately adds, "I think you need some coffee, dude." Pause. "Why are you so angry?"

"I'm out of here, Julian." I start walking away. "As usual, a total mistake."

A blue Jeep follows me from the Beverly Hills Hotel to where the cab drops me off in front of the Doheny Plaza.

Something has changed since I was here seven hours ago. I call the doorman while staring at the desk in my office. The computer is on. It wasn't when I left. I'm staring at the stack of paper next to the computer. When the doorman answers I'm staring at a small knife used to open envelopes that was placed on the stack of paper. It was in a drawer when I headed out to the premiere. I hang the phone up without saying anything. Moving around the condo I ask, "Is anyone here?" I lean over the duvet in the bedroom. I run my hand across it. It smells different. I check the door for the third time. It's locked. I stare at the Christmas tree longer than I should and then I take the elevator down to the lobby.

The night doorman sits at the front desk in the lushly lit lobby. I walk toward him, unsure of what to say. He looks up from a small TV.

"Did someone come by my place?" I ask. "Tonight? While I was out?"

The doorman checks the log. "No. Why?"

"I think there was someone in my place."

"What do you mean?" the doorman asks. "I don't understand."

"I think someone was in my condo while I was out."

"I've been here all night," the doorman says. "No one came by."

I just stand there. The sound of a helicopter roars over the building.

"Anyway, they couldn't get in the elevator without me opening it for them," the doorman says. "Plus Bobby's outside." He motions to the security guard slowly pacing the driveway. "Are you sure someone was in there?" He sounds amused. He notices I'm drunk. "Maybe it was no one," he says.

Pare it down, I warn myself. Put it away. Just pare everything down. Or else the bells will start chiming. "Things were rearranged," I murmur. "My computer was on . . ."

"Is anything missing?" the doorman asks, now openly humoring me. "You want me to call the police?"

In a neutral voice: "No." And then I say it again. "No."

"It's been a quiet night."

"Well . . ." I'm backing away. "That's good."

An actress I met at the casting sessions this morning is having lunch with me at Comme Ça. When she walked into the room at the casting director's complex in Culver City she instantly provided a steady hum of menace that left me dazed, which acted as a mask so I appeared as calm as a cipher. I haven't heard of her agent or the management company that reps her—she came in as someone's favor—and I'm thinking how different things would be if I had. Certain tensions melt away but they're always replaced with new ones. She's drinking a glass of champagne and I still have my sunglasses on and she keeps touching her hair and talking vaguely about her life. She lives in Elysian Park. She's a hostess at the Formosa Café. I twist in my chair while she answers a text. She notices this and then offers an apology. It's not coy, exactly, but it's premeditated. Like everything else she does it wants a reaction.

"So what are you doing for Christmas?" I ask her.

"Seeing my family."

"Will that be fun?"

"It depends." She looks at me quizzically. "Why?"

I shrug. "I'm just interested."

She touches her hair again: blond, blown out. A napkin becomes faintly stained after she wipes her lips with it. I mention the parties I went to last night. The actress is impressed, especially by the one I went to first. She says she had friends who were at that party. She says she wanted to go but she had to work. She wants me to confirm if a certain young actor was there. When I say he was, the expression on her face makes me realize something. She notices.

"I'm sorry," she says. "He's an idiot."

Some people at that party, she adds, are freaks, then mentions a drug I've never heard of, and tells me a story that involves ski masks, zombies, a van, chains, a secret community, and asks me about a Hispanic girl who disappeared in some desert. She drops the name of an actress I've never heard of. I'm trying to stay focused, trying to stay in the moment, not wanting to lose the romance of it all. *Concealed*, a movie I wrote, is brought up. And then I get the connection: she asked about the young actor with the gorgeous girl I was gazing at because he had a small role in *Concealed*.

"I don't really want to know." I'm staring at the traffic on Melrose. "I didn't stay long. I had another party to go to." And suddenly I remember the blond girl walking out of the shadows in Bel Air. I'm surprised she has stayed with me, and that her image has lingered for so long.

"How do you think it went?" she asks.

"I thought you were great," I say. "I told you that."

She laughs, pleased. She could be twenty. She could be thirty. You can't tell. And if you could, everything would be over. Destiny. "Destiny" is the word I'm thinking about. The actress murmurs a line from *The Listeners*. I made sure the director and producer had no interest in her for the role she auditioned for before asking her out. This is the only reason she's with me at lunch and I've been here so many times and I realize there's another premiere tonight and that I'm meeting the producer in Westwood at six. I check my watch. I've kept the afternoon open. The actress drains the glass of champagne. An attentive and handsome waiter fills it up again. I've had nothing to drink because something else in the lunch is working for me. She needs to take this to the next level if anything's ever going to pan out for her.

"Are you happy?" she asks.

Startled, I say, "Yeah. Are you?"

She leans in. "I could be."

"What do you want to do?" I look at her straight on.

We spend an hour in the bedroom in the condo on the fifteenth floor of the Doheny Plaza. That's all it requires.

Afterward she says she feels disconnected from reality. I tell her it doesn't matter. I'm blushing when she tells me how nice my hands are.

The premiere is at the Village and the after-party, elaborate and fanciful, is at the W Hotel. (It was supposed to be at the Napa Valley Grille—because of overcrowding was moved to this less accessible but larger venue.) Forced to watch people pretend to yell and cry for two and a half hours can push you to a dark distance that takes a day to come back from, yet I found the movie well made and coherent (which is always a miracle) even though I often had to think awful thoughts in order to stay awake. I'm standing by the pool talking to a young actress about fasting and her yoga routine and how superstoked she is to be in a movie about human sacrifices, and the initial shyness—apparent in large, soft eyes—is encouraging. But then you say the wrong thing and those eyes reveal an innate distrust mixed with a lingering curiosity that everyone shares out here and she drifts off, and looking up at the hotel, encased in the crowd, clutching my phone, I start counting how many rooms are lit and how many aren't and then realize I've had sex with five different people in this hotel, one of them now dead. I take a piece of sushi from a passing tray. "Well, you did it," I tell the executive who allowed this movie to be made. Daniel Carter, who I've known since we were freshmen at Camden, is the director, but our friendship is worn out and he's been avoiding me. And tonight I see why: he's with Meghan Reynolds, so I can't offer the faked congratulations I prepared. Daniel sold his first script when he was twenty-two and has had no problems with his career since then.

"She's dressed like a teenager," Blair says. "I guess that's because she is one."

I glance over at Blair, then look back across the crowd at Meghan and Daniel.

"I'm not going there with you now."

"We all make choices, right?"

"Your husband hates me."

"No, he doesn't."

"There was a girl at your house, at the party . . ." The need to ask about this is so physical I can't put a halt to it. I turn to Blair. "Never mind."

"I heard you had drinks with Julian last night," Blair says. She's staring at the pool, the title of the movie shimmering on the bottom in giant cursive lettering.

"You *heard*?" I light a cigarette. "How did you *hear* this unless Julian told you?"

Blair doesn't say anything.

"So you're still in touch with Julian?" I ask. "Why?" I pause. "Does Trent know?" Another pause. "Or is that just a . . . detail?"

"What are you trying to say?"

"That I'm surprised you're actually talking to me."

"I just wanted to warn you about him. That's all."

"Warn me? About what?" I ask. "I've been through the whole Julian thing before. I think I can handle it."

"It's not a big hassle," she says. "If you can just do me a favor and not talk to him if he tries to make contact it would make everything a lot easier." And then for emphasis she adds, "I'd appreciate it."

"What's Julian doing these days? There was a rumor he was actually running a teenage hooker service." I pause. "It sounded like old times."

"Look, if you can just do this one thing I'd really appreciate it."

"Is this real? Or is this just an excuse to talk to me again?"

"You could have called. You could have . . ." Her voice trails off.

"I tried," I say. "But you were angry."

"Not angry," she says. "Just . . . disappointed." She pauses. "You didn't try hard enough."

For a few seconds we're both silent and it's a cold and minor variation on so many conversations we've had and I'm thinking about the blond girl on the veranda and I imagine Blair's thinking about the last time I made love to her. This disparity should scar me but doesn't. And then Blair's talking to a guy from CAA and a band begins playing, which I take as my cue to leave, but really it's the text I suddenly get that says *I'm watching you* that pushes me out of the party.

At the valet in front of the hotel, Rip Millar grabs my arm as I'm texting *Who is this?* and I have to yank my arm away since I'm so alarmed by his appearance. I don't recognize Rip at first. His face is unnaturally smooth, redone in such a way that the eyes are shocked open with perpetual surprise; it's a face mimicking a face, and it looks agonized. The lips are too thick. The skin's orange. The hair is dyed yellow and carefully gelled. He looks like he's been quickly dipped in acid; things fell off, skin was removed. It's almost defiantly grotesque. He's on drugs, I'm thinking. He has to be on drugs to look like this. Rip's with a girl so young I mistake her for his daughter but then I remember Rip doesn't have any children. The girl has had so much work done that she looks deformed. Rip had been handsome once and his voice is the same whisper it was when we were nineteen.

"Hey, Clay," Rip says. "Why are you back in town?"

"Because I live here," I say.

Rip's visage calmly scrutinizes me. "I thought you spent most of your time in New York."

"I mean I'm back and forth."

"I heard you met a friend of mine."

"Who?"

"Yeah," he says with a dreadful grin, his mouth filled with teeth that are too white. "I heard you really hit it off."

I just want to leave. The fear is swarming. The black BMW suddenly materializes. A valet holds the door open. The horrible face forces me to glance anywhere but at him. "Rip, I've gotta go." I gesture helplessly at my car.

"Let's have dinner while you're back," Rip says. "I'm serious."

"Okay, but I really have to go now."

"*Descansado*," he tells me.

"What does that mean?"

"*Descansado*," Rip says. "It means 'take it easy,'" he whispers, clutching the child next to him.

"Yeah?"

"It means relax."

It happens again. While waiting for the girl to come over I'm reaching into the refrigerator for a bottle of white wine when I notice that a Diet Coke's missing and that cartons and jars have been rearranged and I'm telling myself this isn't possible, and after looking around the condo for other clues maybe it isn't. It's not until I'm staring at the Christmas tree that I finally hear the bones tapping against the windowpane: one strand of lights not connected to the other strands has been unplugged leaving a jagged black streak within the lit tree. This is the detail that announces: you've been warned. This is the detail that says: they want you to know. I drink a glass of vodka, and then I drink another. *Who is this?* I text. A minute later I receive an answer from a blocked number that annihilates whatever peace the alcohol brought on. *I promised someone I wouldn't tell you.*

I'm walking through the Grove to have lunch with Julian, who texts me that he's at a table next to the Pinkberry in the Farmers Market. *I thought you said I was a total mistake,* he typed back when I e-mailed him earlier. *Maybe you are but I still want to see you* was my reply. I keep ignoring the feeling of being followed. I keep ignoring the texts from the blocked number telling me *I'm watching you.* I tell myself the texts are coming from the dead boy whose condo I bought. It's easier that way. This morning the girl I called over when I got home from the W Hotel was asleep in the bedroom. I woke her up and told her she had to get out because the maid was coming. At the casting sessions it was all boys and though I wasn't exactly bored I didn't need to be there, and songs constantly floating in the car keep commenting on everything neutral encased within the windshield's frame (. . . *one time you were blowing young ruffians* . . . sung over the digital billboard on Sunset advertising the new Pixar movie) and the fear builds into a muted fury and then has no choice but to melt away into a simple and addictive sadness. Daniel's arm around Meghan Reynolds's waist sometimes blocks the view at traffic lights. And then it's the blond girl on the veranda. It's almost always her image now that deflects everything.

Y̶ou knew that Meghan Reynolds was with Daniel," I say. "I saw them last night. You knew I'd been with her over the summer. You also knew she's with Daniel now."

"Everyone knows," Julian says, confused. "So what?"

"I didn't," I say. "Everyone? What does that mean?"

"It means I guess you weren't paying attention."

I move the conversation to the reason I'm here in the Farmers Market with him. I ask him a question about Blair. There's a longish pause. Julian's usual affability gets washed away with that question.

"We were involved, I guess," he finally says.

"You and Blair?"

"Yeah."

"She doesn't want you to talk to me," I say. "She warned me, in fact, not to."

"Blair asked you not to speak to me? She *warned* you?" He sighs. "She must really be hurt."

"Why is she so hurt?"

"Didn't she tell you why?" he asks.

"No," I say. "I didn't ask."

Julian gives me a quick glance tinged with worry, and then it's gone. "Because I started seeing someone else and it was hard for her when I broke it off."

"Who was the girl?"

"She's an actress. She works in this lounge on La Cienega."

"Did Trent know?"

"He doesn't care," Julian says. "Why are you asking that?"

"Because he cared when it was me," I say. "He still hasn't cooled off. I mean, I don't know why." I pause. "Trent has his own . . . proclivities."

"I think that was something else."

"What's . . . something else?"

"That Blair still likes you."

When Julian speaks again his voice becomes more urgent. "Look, they have a family. They have children. They've made it work. I should have never gone there but . . . I never thought I would hurt her." He stops. "I mean, you're the one who always hurt her the most." He pauses before adding, "You're the one who always did."

"Yeah," I say. "This time she didn't talk to me for almost two years."

"My situation was more . . . I don't know, typical. Something you'd expect," Julian says. "The girl I met was a lot younger and . . ." This seems to remind Julian of something. "How did the casting sessions go this morning?"

"How did you know there were casting sessions this morning?"

Julian mentions a friend of his who had auditioned.

"Why do you know twenty-one-year-old actors?" I ask.

"Because I live here," he says. "And he's not twenty-one."

We're standing next to Julian's Audi in the parking lot off of Fairfax. I'm going back to Culver City when he vaguely mentions a meeting, and I realize I haven't asked him anything about his life, but then I don't really care one way or another. I'm about to leave when suddenly I ask him, "What the fuck happened to Rip Millar?"

At the mention of the name Julian's face becomes too calm.

"I don't know," he says. "Why are you asking me?"

"Because he looks freakish," I say. "I actually got scared."

"What are you talking about?"

"He's a horror movie," I say. "I thought he was going to start drooling."

"I heard he inherited a lot of money. His grandparents." Julian pauses. "Real estate investments. He's opening a club in Hollywood . . ." An annoyance I never detected in Julian announces itself. And then Julian casually tells me a story he heard about this secret cult that encouraged members to starve themselves to death—some kind of torture kick, a *how far can you take it?* kind of thing—and that Rip Millar was somehow indirectly connected to them.

"Rip said something about how I'd met a friend of his," I murmur.

"Did he say a name?"

"I didn't ask," I say. "I didn't want to know who it was."

I notice Julian's hand trembling as he runs it lightly over his hair.

"Hey, don't tell Blair we met, okay?" I finally say.

Julian looks at me strangely. "I don't talk to Blair anymore."

I sigh. "Julian, she told me she heard that you and I were at the Polo Lounge the other night."

Julian's expression is so completely innocent that I believe him when he says, "I haven't talked to Blair since June." Julian is totally relaxed. His eyes don't waver. "I haven't had any contact with her for over six months, Clay." He reacts to the expression on my face. "I didn't tell her we were at the Polo Lounge the other night."

On a break and I'm listening to a message Laurie left on my cell phone ("If you're not speaking to me at least tell me why . . ."), then I delete it midway. The rooms of the casting complex surround a pool, and the rooms are filled with the boys and girls auditioning for the three remaining roles. Sudden interest from a rising young actor whose most recent movie "caused a stir in Toronto" has taken one of the available roles off the table, the part of Kevin Spacey's son. Only one boy out of the dozens seen yesterday has met the team's approval for the other male role. Jon, the director, keeps complaining about the girls. Since *The Listeners* is set in the mid-eighties, he's having problems with their bodies. "I don't know what's happening," he says. "These girls are disappearing."

"What do you mean?" the producer asks.

"Too thin. The fake tits don't help."

Jason, the casting director, says, "Well, they *do* help. But I get it."

"I have no idea what you're complaining about," the producer deadpans.

"It all seems so unwholesome," the director says. "And it's not period, Mark."

Talk turns to the actress who passed out while walking to her car after her audition yesterday—stress, malnutrition—and then to the young actor under consideration for Jeff Bridges's son. "What about Clifton?" the director says. Jason tries to move the director's focus to other actors, but the director keeps insisting.

Clifton is the one I lobbied hard for to be in *Concealed*, the one I took back to Doheny when I found out he was dating an actress I'd been interested in and who showed no interest in me since there was nothing I could offer her. It was made clear what Clifton needed to do if he wanted me to lobby for him. The actor eyed me with a chilled-out glare in the lounge of a restaurant on La Cienega. "I'm not looking for a dude," the actor said. "And even if I was, you're not him." In the jovial language of men I suggested that if he didn't comply I would try to make sure he wouldn't get the part. There was so little hesitancy that the moment became even more unsettling than I had initially made it. The actor simply sighed, "Let's roll." I couldn't tell if the indifference was real or faked. He was planning a career. This was a necessary step. It was just another character he was playing in the bedroom on the fifteenth floor of the Doheny Plaza that night. The BlackBerry on the nightstand that kept flashing, the fake tan and the waxed asshole, the dealer in the Valley who never showed up, the drunken complaints about the Jaguar that had to be sold—the details were so common that it could have been anyone. The same actor came in this morning and smiled briefly at me, did a shaky reading, then improved slightly on the second reading. Whenever I saw him at a party or a restaurant he would casually avoid me, even when I offered my condolences about his girlfriend, that young actress I had wanted, who overdosed on her meds. Since she had a small role in a hit TV show her death was recognized.

"He's twenty-four," Jason complains.

"But he's still really cute." The director mentions the whispers about Clifton's sexual orientation, a supposed gig on a porn site years ago, a rumor about a very famous actor and a tryst in Santa Barbara and Clifton's denial in a *Rolling Stone* cover story about the very famous actor's new movie which Clifton had a small part in: "We're so into girls it's ridiculous."

"I've never gotten the gay vibe," the director says. "He butches it up, I guess."

And then we refocus on the girls.

"Who are we seeing next?"

"Rain Turner," someone says.

Curious, I look up from Laurie's messages that I keep deleting and reach for a headshot. Just as I lift it off the table the girl from the veranda at Trent and Blair's house in Bel Air walks in and I have to pretend I'm not trapped. The blue eyes are complementing a light blue V-neck and a navy-blue miniskirt, something a girl would have worn in 1985 when the movie takes place. Immediately introductions are made and the audition happens—bad, strident, one-note, every other line needs to be reread to her by the director—but something else starts happening. Her stare is a gaze, and my gaze back is the beginning of it, and I imagine the future: *Why do you hate me?* I imagine a girl's anguished voice. *What did I ever do to you?* I imagine someone else screaming.

During the audition I look at Rain Turner's IMDb page on my laptop. She reads for another role and I realize with a panic that she'll never get a callback. She's simply another girl who has gotten by on her looks—her currency in this world—and it will not be fun to watch her grow old. These simple facts I know so well still make everything seem freshly complicated to me. Suddenly I get a text—*Quien es?*—and it takes me a while to realize it's from the girl I was flirting with in the Admiral's Club at JFK the afternoon I flew out here. When I look up again I also realize I've never noticed the white Christmas tree standing by the pool or that the Christmas tree is framed within the window next to the wall with the poster for *Sunset Boulevard* on it.

I'm walking Rain to her car outside the offices on Washington Boulevard.

"So, is this the movie you wanted to put me in?" she asks.

"It could be," I say. "I didn't think you recognized me."

"Of course I recognized you."

"I'm flattered." I pause, and then go for it: "Why didn't you introduce yourself to the producer instead? He was at the party."

She smiles as if amazed, then raises an arm to hit me. I back off playfully.

"Are you usually this brazen before cocktail hour?" she asks. "Jeez." She's charming but there's something rehearsed about the charm, something brittle. The amazed smile seems innocent only because something else is always lurking along its borders.

"Or maybe you should have introduced yourself to the director?" I joke.

She laughs. "The director has a wife."

"His wife lives in Australia."

"I heard he doesn't like girls," she stage-whispers.

"So I'm that rare thing?" I say.

"What's that?" she asks, trying to hide a brief moment of confusion.

"The respected screenwriter?" I suggest, half ironic.

"You're also a producer on this movie."

"That's right, I am," I say. "Which part do you want more?"

"Martina," Rain says, immediately focused. "I think I'm better for that, right?"

By the time we get to her car I find out that she lives in an apartment on Orange Grove, off of Fountain, and that she has a roommate, which will make everything much easier. The transparency of the deal: she's good at handling it, and I admire that. Everything she says is an ocean of signals. Listening to her I realize that she's a lot of girls, but which one is talking to me? Which one will be driving back to the apartment on Orange Grove in the green BMW with the vanity plate that reads PLENTY? Which one would be coming to the bedroom in the Doheny Plaza? We exchange numbers. She puts her sunglasses on.

"So, what do you think my chances are?" she asks.

I say, "I think you're going to be a lot of fun."

"How can you tell that I'm going to be a lot of fun?" she asks. "Some people can't handle me."

"Why don't you let me see for myself," I say.

"How do I know you're not crazy?" she asks. "How do I know you're not the craziest dude I've ever met?"

"You'll have to test me out."

"You have my info," she says. "I'll think about it."

"Rain," I say. "That's not your real name."

"Does it matter?"

"Well, it makes me wonder what else isn't real."

"That's because you're a writer," she says. "That's because you make things up for a living."

"And?"

"And"—she shrugs—"I've noticed that writers tend to worry about things like that."

"About what?"

She gets into the car. "Things like that."

D r. Woolf has an office in a nondescript building on Sawtelle. He's my age and deals primarily with actors and screenwriters, the three-hundred-dollar sessions partly covered by Writers Guild health insurance. I was referred last summer by an actor whose stalled career hastened a relapse, and this was in July after the breakdown over Meghan Reynolds entered its most intense stage, and during the first session Dr. Woolf stopped me when I started reading aloud the e-mails from Meghan that I saved on my iPhone, and we proceeded into the Reversal of Desire exercise—*I want pain, I love pain, pain brings freedom*—and one afternoon in August I left midsession in a rage and drove up to Santa Monica Boulevard where I parked in an empty lot and watched a new print of *Contempt* at the Nuart, slouched in the front row slowly crushing a box of candy, and when I came out of the theater I stared at a digital billboard overlooking the parking lot, its image: an unmade bed, the sheets rumpled, a naked body half lit in a darkened room, white Helvetica lettering curved against the color of flesh.

T he nude pics Rain sends me later that afternoon (they come so much sooner than I expected) are either artistic and boring (sepia-toned, shadowy, posed) or sleazy and arousing (on someone's balcony, legs spread, holding a cell phone in one hand and an unlit cigarette in the other; standing next to a blue-sheeted mattress in an anonymous bedroom, fingers splayed against her lower abdomen), but every one of them is an invitation, every one of them plays on the idea that exposure can ensure fame. At the cocktail party in a suite at the Chateau Marmont—where we needed to sign confidentiality agreements in order to attend—no one says anything nearly as interesting as what Rain's pictures promise. The pictures offer a tension, an otherness, that's lacking in the suite overlooking Sunset. It's the same dialogue ("What's happening with *The Listeners*?" "You've been in New York the last four months?" "Why are you so thin?") spoken by the same actors (Pierce, Kim, Alana) and the rooms might as well be empty and my answers to the questions ("Yeah, everyone has been warned about the nudity." "I'm tired of New York." "Different trainer, yoga.") might as well have been made up of distant avian sounds. This is the last party before everyone goes out of town and I'm hearing about the usual spots in Hawaii, Aspen, Palm Springs, various private islands, and the party's being thrown by a British actor staying at the hotel who had played the villain in a comic-book movie I adapted. "Werewolves of London" keeps blaring, a video of a ceremony at the Kodak Theatre keeps replaying itself on TV screens. A horrible story has moved rapidly through town involving a young Hispanic actress whose body was somehow found in a mass grave across the border, and for some reason this is connected to a drug cartel in Tijuana. Mangled bodies were strewn through the pit. Tongues were cut out. And the story gets more outlandish as it keeps being retold: there's now a barrel of industrial acid containing liquefied human remains. A body is now dumped in front of an elementary school as a warning, a taunting message. I keep checking Rain's pics that were sent through earthlink.net from allamericangirlUSA (subject heading: *hey crazy, let's get cracking*) when I'm interrupted by a text from a blocked number.

I'm watching you.

I text back: *Is this the same person?*

I'm staring at a wall, at one of Cindy Sherman's untitled film stills, when I feel the phone vibrate in my hand and the question is answered.

No, this is someone different.

A group of guys booked a table at a new lounge on La Cienega and I allow myself to be invited as I'm waiting for a cab and they're waiting for their cars in front of Bar Marmont and I'm staring up at the parapets of the Chateau and thinking about the year I lived there, after I left the El Royale and before I moved into the Doheny Plaza—the AA meetings on Robertson and Melrose, the twenty-dollar margaritas from room service, the teenager I fucked on the couch in #44—when I see Rip Millar pull up in a convertible Porsche. I hide back in the shadows as Rip shambles toward the hotel clutching a girl in a baby-doll dress by the wrist, and one of the guys calls out something to him and Rip turns his head and makes a sound that passes for laughter and then says in a singsong voice, "Enjoy yourselves." I started with champagne tonight so the lucidity hasn't worn off and the dead zone isn't bleeding forward yet and I'm in someone's Aston Martin and he's bragging about a whore he keeps in his Abbot Kinney condo just east of the Venice canals and another one in a suite at the Huntley. I murmur the hotel's ad line ("Sea and be seen") as we're passing the limousines and gangs of paparazzi outside of Koi and STK, and standing at the curb in front of Reveal I'm staring at the cypress trees looming against the night sky until the two other guys from the party at the Chateau pull up to the valet and I don't really know anyone so everything is comfortable—Wayne's a producer with a deal at Lionsgate that's going nowhere and Kit is an entertainment lawyer at a firm in Beverly Hills. Banks, who drove me, is a creator of reality shows. When I ask Banks why he chose this place, Reveal, he says, "Rip Millar recommended it to me. Rip got us in."

Inside, the place is packed, vaguely Peruvian, voices bouncing off the high ceiling, the amplified sounds of a waterfall splashing somewhere compete with the Beck song booming throughout the lounge. As the owner leads us to our table, two paper-thin girls stop me at the entrance to the dining room and remind me about a night at the Mercer in New York last October. I didn't sleep with either one of them—we were just doing coke and watching *The Hills*—but the guys become enticed. Someone mentions Meghan Reynolds and I tense up.

"It's interesting how much play you get out of this," Kit says, once we're seated at a table in the center of the room. "Isn't it exhausting?"

"That's a question that contains a lot of other questions," I say.

"Have you ever heard the joke about the Polish actress?" Banks asks. "She came to Hollywood and fucked the writer." He pauses, glances at me. "I guess it's not so funny."

"Be in my screenplay and I'll make you a star," Kit says in a baby voice.

"Clay obviously doesn't underestimate the desperation factor in this town," Wayne says.

"In a place where there's so much bitterness," Banks says with a light touch, "anything is possible, right?"

"*Possible?* Hey, I just think it's kind of unbelievable." Kit shrugs.

"I think Clay is very pragmatic," Banks says. "What's unbelievable is clinging to a fading belief in love, Kit." He pauses. "But that's just me."

"I mean, you're a nice-looking guy for your age," Kit says to me, "but you don't really have the clout."

Banks considers this. "I guess people find this out sooner or later, right?"

"Yeah, but they're always replaced, Banks," Wayne says. "On a daily basis there's a whole new army of the retarded eager to be defiled."

"You guys don't need to remind me that I'm not really a player . . . but I can be useful, I guess." I'm sighing, staying loose. "Just always make sure you have some kind of producer credit. Stay friendly with the director. Get to know casting agents. It all helps the cause." I pause for effect before adding, "I'm very patient."

"It's a plan," Kit says. "It's very, um, subtle."

"It's a philosophy," someone else says.

"It's just how I roll."

Wayne looks up, taking note of my uninflected voice.

"I guess it kind of makes sense. You've been involved in some high-profile hits," Wayne mutters, "for what it's worth."

Kit leans forward. "It's just not a very good way to make friends."

Banks closes his menu when the owner leans down and whispers something to him. Josh Hartnett, who was going to play one of the sons in *The Listeners* and then bailed, walks over and crouches by the bamboo chair and we have a brief exchange about another script of mine that he's been circling, but his apologetic lack of commitment only makes me seem more remote than I'm actually feeling. Though I know that what he's saying isn't true I smile and agree anyway. Austere plates of raw fish start arriving, along with ice-cold bottles of premium sake, and then the guys make fun of a very successful shark movie I wrote, and the series about witches I created that ran for two seasons on Showtime, then Wayne starts telling a story about an actress who stalked him until he cast her in a movie about a monster that looked like a talking beanbag. Just as the owner sends the table a complimentary dessert—an elaborate plate of sugared doughnuts drizzled with caramel—the night begins sliding into its last act. I'm scanning the room when I see the cascade of blond hair, the wide-open pale blue eyes, the dumb smile that offsets her beauty while at the same time making it more pronounced: she's on the phone at the hostess stand. And then I realize it's time to cross the line.

I knew you were here," Rain says.

"Why didn't you say something?" I ask, sobering up immediately in her presence. "You could have sent over a few cocktails."

"I assumed you guys were already wasted when you came in."

"Why didn't you say hello?"

"I was seating a table," she says. "Plus the owner likes to impress Banks."

"So, this is where you work?"

"Yes," she purrs. "Glamorous, isn't it?"

"You seem happy."

"I am," she says. "I'm almost afraid of how happy I am."

"Come on, don't be afraid."

She mimics a little girl. "Well, I could always be happier."

"Well," I say contemplatively. "I got your pics."

When I get back to the Doheny Plaza, waiting for Rain to come over after she finishes her shift, I sit in my office checking Rain's IMDb page again, studying it for clues. There are no credits for the last two years, stopping abruptly after "Christine" in a Michael Bay movie and "Stacy's Friend" in an episode of *CSI: Miami* and then I'm filling in the missing pieces, the things she doesn't want anyone to know. The credits begin when Rain must have been eighteen. I'm doing the math by guessing—the date of birth has been shaved by at least a couple years and I'm putting her age at probably twenty-two or twenty-three. She was at the University of Michigan (cheerleader for the Wolverines, "studying medicine") but no dates are given (if she attended at all) so it's hard to confirm exactly how old she is. Though Rain would say it doesn't matter. Rain would argue that just the idea of her in a cheerleader's uniform is enough. But the fact that there are no photos of her as a cheerleader causes more whispers in that darkly lit hallway, and the addition of "studying medicine" makes the whispering even louder.

The most recent information: Rain posted a month ago that she was listed as one of *L.A. Confidential*'s most eligible singles in the December issue, and so is—I notice unsurprisingly enough when I pull up the magazine online— Amanda Flew, the actress I hit on at JFK and who texted me during Rain's audition. The photo of Rain in *L.A. Confidential* is the same headshot that obviously is Rain's preferred image of herself: staring blankly at the camera so that her perfect features can speak for themselves, but there's the beginning of a slight grin she almost manages to make suggestive of an intelligence that the cleavage and her career choice otherwise argue against. And it doesn't matter if any intelligence actually exists because it's really about the look, the idea of a girl like this, the promise of sex. It's all about the lure. The MySpace page reveals nothing to me at first except that her favorite band is the Fray. "How to Save a Life" plays when you open the page. I'm about to scan it when I get a text from a blocked number.

I look down at the phone on my desk.

The screen says: *I'm watching you.*

Instead of ignoring it and turning away, I text back: *Where am I?*

Within the time it takes another text to arrive I've already walked to the kitchen and poured myself a glass of vodka. When I reach for the phone back in my office I freeze.

You're at home.

I hold the phone away from my face and glance out the window.

And then I text back: *No I'm not.*

It takes a minute before the phone flashes a glow that tells me I have a response.

I can see you, the text reads. *U r standing in your office.*

I glance out the window again and am surprised when I find myself backing into a wall. The condo suddenly seems so empty but it isn't—there are voices in it, and they linger like they always do—and I turn off the lights and slowly move to the balcony, and beneath the wavering fronds of a palm tree, the blue Jeep is parked on the corner of Elevado, and then I turn the lights back on and move to the front door and open it and stare down the empty Art Deco hallway, and then I'm walking toward the elevators.

I pass the night doorman and push the lobby doors open and then I'm walking quickly past the security guard and then I stumble into a jog toward Elevado and just as I turn the corner the Jeep's headlights flash their high beams, immediately blinding me. The Jeep peels away from the curb and it causes a van coming up Doheny to swerve as the Jeep makes a right and lurches toward Sunset and when I look up I'm standing exactly where the Jeep was parked and can see the lights of my condo through the branches of the trees, and except for the occasional car cruising by, it's dark and soundless on Elevado. I keep my eyes on the windows of my empty office as I walk back to the Doheny Plaza fifteen stories up, a place I was standing in just moments ago, being watched by whoever was in the blue Jeep, and I realize I'm panting as I walk past the security guard, and I slow down, trying to catch my breath, and smile at him, but as I'm about to head inside a green BMW pulls up.

I love the view," Rain says, holding a tumbler of tequila, standing on the balcony overlooking the city. I'm staring past her down at the empty space on Elevado where the Jeep was parked and it's three in the morning and I come up behind her and down below the wind gently drapes palm fronds over the rippling water of the Doheny Plaza's lit pool and the only light in the condo comes from the Christmas

tree in the corner and Counting Crows' "A Long December" plays softly in the background.

"Don't you have a boyfriend?" I ask. "Someone . . .
more age-appropriate than me?"

"Guys my age are idiots," she says, turning around.
"Guys my age are awful."

"I have news for you," I say, leaning into her. "So are
guys my age."

"But you look good for your age," she says, stroking
my face. "You look ten years younger," she says. "You've
had work done, right?" Her fingers keep combing the hair
that had been dyed the week before. Her other hand runs
along the sleeve of the T-shirt with the skateboard logo on
it. In the bedroom she lets me go down on her and after I
make her come she lets me slide in.

During the last week of December if we aren't in bed
we're at the movies or watching screeners and Rain simply
nods when I tell her everything that's wrong with the movie
we've just seen and she doesn't argue back. "I liked it," she
will say, putting a light touch on everything, her upper lip
always provocatively lifted, her eyes always drained of
intent, programmed not to be challenging or negative. This
is someone trying to stay young because she knows that
what matters most to you is the youthful surface. This is
supposed to be part of the appeal: keep everything young
and soft, keep everything on the surface, even with the
knowledge that the surface fades and can't be held together
forever—take advantage before the expiration date appears

in the nearing distance. The surface Rain presents is really all she's about, and since so many girls look like Rain another part of the appeal is watching her try to figure out why I've become so interested in her and not someone else.

"Am I the only one you're interested in?" she asks. "I mean right now, for the part?"

My eyes scan the bedroom we're lying in until they land on hers. "Yes."

"Why?" And then a teasing smile. "Why me?"

This question and my subsequent nonanswer leave her wanting to impart information that, in the bedroom on the fifteenth floor of the Doheny Plaza, has no reason to even exist. You ignore why she left Lansing at seventeen and the casual hints of an abusive uncle (a made-for-sympathy move that threatens to erase the carnality) and why she dropped out of the University of Michigan (I don't ask whether she'd ever enrolled) and what led to the side trips to New York and Miami before she landed in L.A. and you don't ask what she must have done with the photographer who discovered her when she was waitressing at the café on Melrose or about the career modeling lingerie that probably seemed promising at nineteen and that led to the commercials that led to a couple of tiny roles in films and definitely not putting all her hopes into the third part of a horror franchise that panned into nothing and then it was the quick slide into the bit parts on TV shows you've never heard of, the pilot shot but never aired, and covering everything else is the distant humiliation of bartending gigs and the favors that got her the hostess job at Reveal. Decoding everything, you piece together the agent who ignores her. You begin to understand through her muted complaints that the management company no longer cares. Her need is so immense that you become surrounded by it; this need is so enormous that you realize you can actually control it, and I know this because I've done it before.

We sit in my office naked, buzzed on champagne, while she shows me pics from a Calvin Klein show, audition tapes a friend shot, a modeling portfolio, paparazzi photos of her at B-list events—the opening of a shoe store on Canon, a charity benefit at someone's home in Brentwood, standing with a group of girls at the Playboy Mansion at the Midsummer Night's Dream Party—and then always it seems we're back in the bedroom.

"What do you want for Christmas?" she asks.

"This. You." I smile. "What do you want?"

"I want a part in your movie," she says. "You know that."

"Yeah?" I ask, my hand tracing her thigh. "*My* movie? Which part?"

"I want the part of Martina." She kisses me, her hand moving down to my cock, gripping it, releasing it, gripping it again.

"And I'm going to try and get it for you."

The pause is involuntary but she recovers in a second. "*Try?*"

If we aren't in bed or watching movies we're at the Bristol Farms down the street buying champagne or at the Apple store in the Westfield Mall in Century City because she needs a new computer and also wants an iPhone ("It's Christmas," she purrs as if it matters) and I'll hand the BMW over to the valet at the mall and notice the looks from the guys taking the car, and the stares from so many other men roaming the mall, and she notices them too and walks quickly, pulling me along, while talking mindlessly to no one on her cell phone, a self-protective gesture, a way to combat the stares by not acknowledging them. These stares are always the grim reminders of a pretty girl's life in this town, and though I've been with other beautiful women, the neurosis about their looks had already hardened into a kind of bitter acceptance that Rain doesn't seem to share. One of the last afternoons together that December, we're heading to the Apple store drunk on champagne, Rain nestling into me, wearing Yves Saint Laurent sunglasses as we walk beneath the overcast sky looming above the towers of Century City, the chiming bells of Christmas carols everywhere, and she's happy because we'd just watched her reel, which includes the two scenes she was in from a Jim Carrey movie, a drama that tanked. (After squinting hard at the screen, I enthusiastically complimented her and then asked why she hadn't listed the movie on her résumé, and she admitted the scenes were cut.) She's still asking me if I'm telling the truth about her scenes as we move toward the Apple store and I assure her that I am instead of admitting how dismaying the performance actually was. There was no way those scenes should have been kept in the movie—the decision to remove them was the correct one. (I have to stop myself from wondering how she got the part, because that would be entering a maze with no escape.) What keeps me interested—and it always does—is how can she be a bad actress on film but a good one in reality? This is where the suspense of it all usually lies. And later, for the first time since Meghan Reynolds, I think hopefully—lying in bed, lifting a glass filled with champagne to my lips, her face hovering above mine—that maybe she isn't acting with me.

We're shopping at the Bristol Farms on Doheny for another case of champagne in the last week of December when I lose her in one of the aisles and I become dazed when I realize that the market used to be Chasen's, the restaurant I came to with my parents on various Christmas Eves, when I was a teenager, and I try to reconfigure the restaurant's layout while standing in the produce section, "Do They Know It's Christmas?" playing throughout the store, and when nothing comes it's a sad relief. And then I notice Rain's gone and I'm moving through the aisles and I'm thinking about pictures of her naked on a yacht, my hand between her legs, my tongue on her cunt while she comes and then I find her outside, leaning against my BMW talking to a handsome guy I don't recognize, his arm in a sling, and he walks away as I wheel my cart toward them and when I ask her who he was she smiles reassuringly and says "Graham" and then "No one" and then "He's a magician."

I kiss her on the mouth. She looks nervously around. I watch her reflection in the window of the BMW. "What's wrong?" I ask. "Not here," she says, but as if "not here" is a promise of somewhere better. The deserted parking lot is suddenly freezing, the icy air so cold it shimmers.

During that week we spend together things aren't completely tracking—there are lapses—but she acts like it doesn't matter, which helps cause the fear to fade away. Rain replaces it with something else that's easy to lose yourself in, despite, for example, the fact that a few of my friends still in town wanted to get together for dinner at Sona but the invitation caused a low-level anxiety in Rain that seemed alien to her nature and this became briefly revealing. ("I don't want to be with anyone else but you" is her excuse.) But the lapses and evasions aren't loud—Rain is still soothing enough for the texts from the blocked numbers to stop arriving and for the blue Jeep to disappear along with my desire to start work again on any number of projects I'm involved with and the long brooding silences are gone and the bottle of Viagra in the nightstand drawer is left untouched and the ghosts rearranging things in the condo have taken flight and Rain makes me believe this is something with a future. Rain convinces me that this is really happening. Meghan Reynolds fades into a blur because Rain demands that the focus be on her, and because everything about her works for me I don't even realize it when it slips into something beyond simply working and for the first time since Meghan Reynolds I make the mistake of starting to care. But there's one dark fact humming loudly over everything that I keep trying to ignore but can't because it's the only thing that keeps the balance in place. It's the thing that doesn't let me fall completely away. It's the thing that saves me from collapsing: she's too old for the part she thinks she's going to get.

S o when will you help me?" she asks while we're sitting in the café down the street from the Doheny Plaza, idling over a late breakfast, both of us floating away from hangovers with the dope we smoked and Xanax. "I think you should make the calls as soon as possible," she says, looking at herself in a mirror. "Right when everybody comes back, okay?" I'm smiling at her serenely and nodding. I ignore the creases of suspicion on her face even after I remove my sunglasses, and then I assure her with a "Yes" followed by a warm kiss.

T his assumed peace lasts only about a week. There's always the possibility of something frightening happening, and then it usually does. Two days before Kelly Montrose's body is found, Rain wakes up and mentions she had a dream that night. I'm already up, taking pictures of her while she sleeps, and now that she's awake she flinches when I take another one and she says that in her dream she saw a young man in my kitchen, a boy, really, but old enough to be desirable, and he was staring at her and there was dried blood crusted above his upper lip and there was a blurred tattoo of a dragon etched on his forearm and the boy told her he had wanted to live here in 1508, but the boy told her not to worry, that he was lucky, and then his face turned black and he bared his teeth and then he was dust, and I tell Rain about the party boy who had owned this apartment and I tell her that the building is haunted, that at night vampires hide in the palm trees surrounding the building waiting for the lights to go out, and then roam the hallways, and finally the camera gets her attention and she's animated and I keep flashing the camera, my head propped on a pillow while she glances at the flat-screen TV—a shot of people running from a jungle, an episode of *Lost,* and I reach for a Corona on the nightstand. "The vampires don't roam the hallways," she finally murmurs, recovered. "The vampires own the units." And then we run lines for the part of Martina in *The Listeners.*

Kelly Montrose was rumored to be with the Hispanic actress who had been found in the mass grave right before Christmas. The last sighting of him was on a tennis court in Palm Springs one afternoon in mid-December. Kelly's naked body was smeared across a highway in Juárez and then propped against a tree. Two other men were found nearby entombed in blocks of cement. Kelly's face was peeled off, and his hands were missing. There was a note pinned to his body revealing nothing: *cabron? cabron? cabron?* Things I didn't know about Kelly: the crystal meth thing, the stepmother who died during plastic surgery, the supposed connections with the drug cartel. This discovery feels only tangential since I never really knew Kelly Montrose—he produced movies, I'd met him several times about various projects—and he was never close enough to anyone I knew to define any of my relationships. Rain spends the day before Kelly Montrose is found at a distance: pacing the balcony, texting, taking calls, returning calls, increasingly agitated, leaning against the railing, gazing past the plunge of the balcony at a couple of guys jogging shirtless on the street below. When I ask her what's wrong she keeps blaming her family. I keep dragging her back to the bedroom and she's always resisting, promising "In a minute, in a minute . . ." After downing two shots of tequila she lazes on the balcony in just a thong, ignoring the helicopter swooping above her, and that night in the dark bedroom in the Doheny Plaza, drunk on margaritas, candles glowing around her while I complain about another movie playing on the giant flat screen, Rain can't help it and for the first time something causes her to tune out and when I finally notice, my voice starts to waver and as I fade into silence she simply asks, without looking over at me, in a neutral voice, her eyes gazing at the TV, "What's the worst thing you've ever done?"

I have to go to San Diego," she says.

I'm just waking up, squinting at the light pouring into the bedroom. The shades have been pulled up and she's walking around in the brightness of the room collecting things.

"What time is it?" I ask.

"Almost noon."

"What are you doing?"

"I have to go to San Diego," she says. "Something's come up."

I reach out for her, trying to pull her back onto the bed.

"Clay, stop. I have to go."

"Why? Who are you seeing down there?"

"My mother," she mutters. "My crazy fucking mother."

"What's wrong?" I ask. "What happened?"

"Nothing. The usual. Whatever. I'll call you when I get there."

"When am I going to see you again?"

"When I get back."

"When are you getting back?"

"I don't know. Soon. A couple of days."

"Are you okay?" I ask. "You seemed kind of freaked out yesterday."

"No, I'm better," she says. "I'm okay."

To placate me she kisses me on the mouth. "I had a nice time," she says, stroking my face, and the sound of the air-conditioning competes with the big smile and then the smile and the cool air become in the drift of things suddenly amplified, almost frantic, and I pull her toward me onto the bed and I press my face against her thighs and inhale and then I try to flip her over but she gently pushes me away. I lower the sheet, revealing my hard-on, and she aims for levity and rolls her eyes. I can suddenly see my reflection in a mirror in the corner of the bedroom: an old-looking teenager. She gets up and scans the room to see if she's forgotten anything. I reach for the camera on the nightstand

and start taking pictures of her. She's staring into a Versace bag that had once been filled with packets of cocaine, the other thing that had fueled so much of the sex, the thing that helped make the fantasy seem much more discrete and innocent than it really was, the thing that made it seem as if the desire was reciprocated. "Could you call the valet and have him bring my car up?" she asks, frowning as she checks a text.

"I don't want you to go."

"I said I'll be back," she murmurs absently.

"Don't make me beg," I say. "I'm warning you."

"Even if you did it wouldn't work." She doesn't look up when she says this.

"Can I come with you?"

"Stop it."

"I'm imagining things."

"Don't."

"I'm imagining there are many versions of this event."

"Event? I'm going to fucking San Diego to see my fucking mother."

"Neither one of us wants to admit that something's wrong," I murmur, snapping another pic.

"You just did." She briefly poses. Another flash.

"Rain, I'm serious—"

"Stop turning this into a drama, Crazy." Again: the sly smile.

"Drama?" I ask innocently. "Who? Me?"

The last thing she says before she leaves: "Will you make sure I get that callback?"

The digital billboards glowing in the gray haze all seem to say *no* and the poinsettias lining the median at Sunset Plaza are dying and fog keeps enveloping the towers in Century City and the world becomes a science-fiction movie—because none of it really has anything to do with me. It's a world where getting stoned is the only option. Everything becomes more vague and abstract since every desire and every whim that had been catered to constantly in that last week of December is now gone and I don't want to replace it with anyone else because there's no substitute—the teen porn sites seem different, repainted somehow, nothing kicks in, it doesn't work anymore—and so I re-create almost hourly in my mind the sex that happened in the bedroom over those eight days she was here and when I try to outline a script that I've been lazy about it comes out half sincere and half ironic because Rain's failure to return calls or text back becomes a distraction and then, only three days after she leaves, it officially becomes an obstacle. The bruises on my chest and arms, the imprints from Rain's fingers and the scratches on my shoulders and thighs, begin to fade and I stop returning various e-mails from people back in town because I have no desire to gossip about Kelly Montrose or dis the awards buzz or hear about people's plans for Sundance and I have no reason to go back to the casting sessions in Culver City (because what I want has already happened) and without Rain here it all dissipates entirely and the calm becomes impossible, something I can't control. And so I find myself in Dr. Woolf's office on Sawtelle and the pattern

that keeps repeating itself is again pointed out and its reasons are located and we practice techniques to lessen the
pain. And just when I think I'm going to be able to deal
with everything a blue Jeep with tinted windows passes me
on Santa Monica while I'm crossing the intersection at
Wilshire. An hour later I get a text from a blocked number,
the first in almost eleven days: *Where did she go?*

Rumors of a video of Kelly Montrose's "execution"—
that it had been circulating on the Web and seen by "reliable
sources"—spreads within the community early one morning in the first week of January. There was supposedly a link
somewhere that led to another link but the first link had
been pulled and there's nothing to find except people on
various blogs debating the video's "authenticity." Supposedly there was a headless body in a black windbreaker hung
from a bridge, a bleak desert lined with scrub brush beneath
it, police tape whipping in the dry wind, and someone else
wrote that the murder was set in a "laboratory" outside of
Juárez and someone else countered with certainty that the
murder was committed in a soccer field by men wearing
hoods and someone else wrote *No, Kelly Montrose was killed
in an abandoned cemetery.* But there's nothing to substantiate
any of it. Someone posted a picture of a severed head grinning broadly from the passenger seat of a bullet-ridden
SUV but it isn't Kelly. In fact there are no shots of him
being pulled along a highway bound with rope, no close-ups
of skin being peeled off a face, no shots of a pair of hands
being amputated while mariachi music is scored over the

images, and after the excitement peaks and the justification for the gossip surrenders to reality the rumors about the Kelly Montrose clips fade into a twilight stage.

But I don't care. After searching for the links I simply fall back into the habit of looking at all the pics Rain sent me and remember the promises I made that didn't involve *The Listeners* but were about agents and about movies with titles like *Boogeyman 2* and *Bait* and I remind her of them in texts I send—*Hey I talked to Don and Braxton* and *Nate wants to rep you* and *Come back and we'll go over your part* and *I'm talking you up to EVERYONE*—that are only answered in the middle of the night: *Hey Crazy that all sounds super!* and *I'll be back soon!!* dotted with emoticons. Unlike everyone else it's not Kelly Montrose that causes my fear to return. It's officially back and because of Rain's absence no longer a faint distraction. And then it's the blue Jeep that passed me on Santa Monica materializing nightly on the corner of Elevado and one night while I watch it dully from my office window it finally pulls away from the curb. And that's when I notice for the first time another car, a black Mercedes, slowly pulling away from a spot farther down the street and following the Jeep onto Doheny and then up to Sunset. From the apartment below Union Square, Laurie has stopped contacting me completely.

What did you do over the holidays?" Rip Millar asks me when a number I don't recognize shows up on my phone and I answer it impulsively, thinking it might be Rain. After

I mention a few family appearances and that basically I just hung around and worked, Rip offers, "My wife wanted to go to Cabo. She's still there." A long silence plays itself out. I'm forced to fill the silence with, "What have you been doing?" Rip describes a couple of parties he seemed to have fun at and then the minor hassles of opening a club in Hollywood and a futile meeting with a city councilman. Rip tells me he's lying in bed watching CNN on his laptop, images of a mosque in flames, ravens flying against the scarlet sky.

"I want to see you," he says. "Have a drink, grab some lunch."

"Can't we just talk over the phone?"

"No," he says. "We need to see each other in person."

"Need?" I ask. "There's something you *need* to see me about?"

"Yeah," he says. "There's something we need to talk about."

"I'm going back to New York soon," I say.

"When are you going back?"

"I don't know." I pause. "I have some things I need to finish up here first and . . ."

"Yeah," he murmurs. "I guess you have your reasons to stay." Rip lets it hang there before adding, "But I think you'll be pretty interested in what I have to tell you."

"I'll check my schedule and let you know."

"*Schedule?*" he asks. "That's funny."

"Why is that funny?" I ask back. "I'm really busy."

"You're a writer. What do you mean, *busy?*" His voice had been slack but now it isn't. "Who have you been hanging out with?"

"I'm . . . at the casting sessions pretty much all day."

A pause before "Really." It's not a question.

"Look, Rip, I'll be in touch."

Rip follows this with, "Well, how is *The Listeners* coming along?"

"It's coming along." I'm straining. "It's very . . . busy."

"Yeah, you're very busy. You already said that."

Move it out of this realm, make it impersonal, concentrate on gossip, anything to elicit sympathy so we can get off the phone. I try another tactic: "And I'm really stressed about what happened to Kelly. It really stressed me out."

Rip pauses. "Yeah? I heard about that." He pauses again. "I didn't know you two were close."

"Yeah. We were pretty close."

The sound Rip makes after I say this is like a muffled giggle, a private riddle whose answer amused him.

"I guess he found himself in a slightly improbable situation. Who knows what kind of people he got involved with?" He gives both sentences a syncopated rhythm.

I pull the phone away from my ear and stare at it until I'm calm enough to bring it back. There's nothing to say.

"That's what happens when you get involved with the wrong element" is all Rip offers, his voice crawling toward me.

"What's the wrong element?"

A pause and then Rip's voice becomes, for the first time I can remember, vaguely annoyed. "Do you really have to ask me that, Clay?"

"Look, Rip, I'll get in touch."

"Yeah, do that. I think the sooner you hear this, the better."

"Why don't you just tell me now?"

"Because it's . . . intimate," Rip says. "Yeah. It's a very intimate thing."

Later that week I'm roaming the fifth floor of the Barneys on Wilshire, stoned, constantly checking my iPhone for messages from Rain that never appear, glancing at the price tags on the sleeves of shiny shirts, things to show off in, unable to concentrate on anything but Rain's absence, and in the men's department I can't even keep up the most rudimentary conversation with a salesman over a Prada suit and I end up at the bar in Barney Greengrass ordering a Bloody Mary and drinking it with my sunglasses on. Rip is having lunch with Griffin Dyer and Eric Thomas, a city councilman who resembles a lifeguard, and whom Rip had been complaining about but now seems friendly with, and Rip's wearing a skull T-shirt he's too old for and baggy Japanese pants and he shakes my hand and when he sees the Bloody Mary and that I'm alone he murmurs, "So, you're really busy, huh?"

Behind him I can feel the burning wind coming in from the patio. Rip's shocked-open eyes are bloodshot and I notice how muscular his arms are.

"Yeah."

"Sitting here? Brooding at Barneys?"

"Yeah." I shift on the bar stool and grip the icy glass.

"Getting a little scruffy there."

I touch my cheek, surprised at how thick the stubble is and by how long it's been since I shaved and I quickly do the math: the day after Rain left.

"Yeah."

The orange face contemplates something and as it leans into me it says, "You're so much further out there than I thought, dude."

A trainer at Equinox introduces himself after I noticed him gazing at me while I work out with my trainer and asks me if I'd like to have coffee with him at Caffe Primo next door to the gym. Cade is wearing a black T-shirt with the word TRAINER on it in small block letters and he has full lips and a white smile and wide blue eyes and carefully groomed stubble and he smells clean, almost antiseptic, and his voice manages to sound both cheerful and hostile at the same time and he's sucking on a water bottle filled with a reddish liquid and sitting in a way that makes you realize he's waiting for someone to notice him and beneath the shade of an umbrella strewn with Christmas lights I'm staring at the traffic on Sunset as we sit at an outdoor table and I'm thinking about the beautiful boy on the treadmill wearing the I STILL HAVE A DREAM T-shirt and realize that it might not have been ironic.

"I read *The Listeners,*" Cade says, glancing away from his cell phone, a text that had been bothering him.

"Really?" I sip my coffee and offer a tight smile, unsure of why I'm here.

"Yeah, a buddy of mine auditioned for the role of Tim."

"Cool," I say. "Are you auditioning?"

"I'd like to," Cade says. "Do you think you can get me in?"

"Oh," I say, now getting it. "Yeah. Sure."

Softly and with a rehearsed shyness he says, "Maybe we can hang out sometime."

"Like . . . when?" I'm momentarily confused.

"Like, I don't know, just hang," he says. "Maybe go to a concert, see a band . . ."

"Yeah, that sounds cool."

Young girls walk by in a trance holding yoga mats, the scent of patchouli and rosemary breezing over us, the glimpse of a butterfly tattoo on a shoulder, and I'm so keyed up about not talking to Rain in almost five days that I keep expecting a car to crash on Sunset because everything seems imminent with disaster and Cade keeps posing constantly as if he'd been photographed his entire life and in front of the H&M store across the plaza men are rolling out a short red carpet.

"Why did you come to me?" I ask Cade.

"Someone pointed you out," he says.

"No, I mean, why me? Why not someone else connected with the movie?"

"Well . . ." Cade tries to figure out why I'm playing it like this. "I heard you help people."

"Yeah?" I ask. "Who told you that?" The question sounds like a dare. The way it sounds forces Cade to be more open with me than he might have been.

"I think you know him."

"Who?"

"Julian. You know Julian Wells, right?"

I tense up even though he said the name innocently.

But suddenly Cade is someone different because of his connection to Julian.

"Right," I say. "How do you know Julian?"

"I worked for him briefly."

"Doing what?"

Cade shrugs. "Personal stuff."

"Like an assistant?"

Cade smiles and turns away and then looks back at me, trying not to seem too concerned by the question. "Yeah, I guess."

Blair calls to invite me to a dinner party she's hosting in Bel Air next week and I'm suspicious at first but when she says it's for Alana's birthday I understand why I'm being invited and the conversation is mellow and tinged with forgiveness and after talking about simple things it feels easy enough to ask, "Can I bring someone?" even though a brief pause on Blair's part forces me back to the past.

"Yeah, sure," she says casually. "Who?"

"Just a friend. Someone I'm working with."

"Who is it?" she asks. "Do I know them?"

"She's an actress," I say. "Her name's Rain Turner."

Blair is silent. Whatever we had recovered earlier in the phone call is now gone.

"She's an actress," I repeat. "Hello?"

Blair doesn't say anything.

"Blair?"

"Look, I thought maybe you'd come solo, but I don't

want her here," she says quickly. "I would never have allowed her to come here."

"Why not?" I ask in a warning voice. "Do you know her?"

"Look, Clay—"

"Oh, fuck this," I say. "Why would you invite me anyway, Blair? What are you doing? Are you trying to fuck with me? Are you still pissed? It's been over two years, Blair."

After a pause, she says, "I think we should talk."

"About what?"

She pauses again. "Meet me somewhere."

"Why can't we talk now?"

"We can't talk over the phone."

"Why not, Blair?"

"Because none of these lines are secure."

Turning off Sunset onto Stone Canyon I drive into the darkness of the canyons and valet park the BMW at the Hotel Bel-Air. I walk across the bridge past the swans floating in the pond and make my way to the dining room but Blair's not there and when I ask the hostess I find out she didn't make a reservation and outside I look around the patio but she's not there either and I'm about to call her when I realize I don't have her number. As I walk to the front desk I'm suddenly aware of how much effort I made to look nice even though nothing was going to happen. The receptionist tells me what room Mrs. Burroughs is in.

I pace around the grounds debating something and

then I give up and walk to the room and knock. When Blair opens the door I walk in past her.

"What are you doing?" I ask.

"What do you mean?"

"It's not going to happen."

"What's not going to happen?"

"This." I make a tired gesture with my arm across the suite.

"That's not why we're . . ." She looks away.

Blair's wearing loose cotton pants and she has no makeup on and her hair's pulled back and whatever work she has had done you can't tell and she's sitting on the edge of the bed next to a Michael Kors bag and she's not wearing her wedding ring.

"It's just a suite that Trent keeps," she says.

"Yeah?" I say, pacing. "Where's Trent?"

"He's still upset about Kelly Montrose," Blair says. "They were close. Trent represented him for a while." She pauses. "Trent's helping plan the memorial."

"What did you think was going to happen?" I ask. "Why am I here?"

"I don't know why you keep—"

"It's not going to happen, Blair."

"You can stop saying that, Clay," she says, an edge in her voice. "I know."

I open the minibar. I don't even look at what bottle I take out. Annoyed, shaky, I pour myself a drink.

"But why wouldn't it happen?" Blair asks. "Is it because of her? The girl you wanted to bring to my house?" She pauses. "The actress?" She pauses again. "You don't think I'd be upset about that?"

"What do you want to talk about?" I ask impatiently.

"I guess in a way it's about Julian."

"Yeah? What about him?" I down the drink. "You were having an affair with him? You guys hooked up? What?"

When Blair bites her lower lip she's eighteen again.

"Julian told you?" she asks. "Is that how you know?"

"I'm just guessing, Blair," I say. "You told me to stay away from him, remember?" And then: "What does it matter? It's been over for a year, right?"

"Did you know that he broke it off?" she asks haltingly.

"Blair, I don't know anything, okay?"

"He broke it off because of that girl."

"What girl?"

"Clay, please don't make this any weirder—"

"I don't know what girl you're talking about."

"I'm talking about the girl you wanted to bring to the dinner party," she says. "That's who he left me for." She pauses again for emphasis. "That's who he's with now."

I break the silence by saying, "You're lying."

"Clay—"

"You're lying because you want me here and—"

"Stop it," she shouts.

"But I don't know what you're saying."

"Rain. Her name's Rain Turner. That's the girl you wanted to bring, right? When Julian broke it off with me she was the reason. They've been together ever since." Again she pauses for effect. "He's still with her."

"How . . . do you know this?" I ask. "I thought you didn't talk to him."

"I don't talk to Julian," she says, "but I know they're together."

I throw the glass against the wall.

Blair looks away, embarrassed.

"You're that upset over her? I mean how long have you even been with her?" Blair asks, her voice cracking. "A couple of weeks?"

Concentrating on the flower arrangement in the middle of the suite is my only hope of focusing while Blair continues.

"I made Trent take her on as a client because Julian asked me to, without telling me he was seeing her. It was a favor I did for him. I thought she was just a friend. Another actress who needed help . . . I did it because . . ." She stops. "Because I liked Julian."

I'm murmuring to myself. "That's why she was at your house."

Blair realizes something after I say this. "You never asked her why she was there, did you?" Another silence. "Jesus, it's still all about you, isn't it? Didn't you ever wonder what the hell she was doing there?" Blair's voice keeps climbing. "Do you know *anything* about her except how she makes *you* feel?"

"I don't believe any of this."

"Why not?"

"Because . . . she's with me."

Finally, I stagger toward the door.

"Wait," Blair says quietly. "I better leave first."

"What does it matter?" I ask, wiping my face.

"Because I think I'm being followed."

I text Rain: *If I don't hear from you I'm going to make them give the part to someone else.* In a matter of minutes I get a text from her. *Hey Crazy, I'm back! Let's hang. Xo.*

In my office, sitting at my desk pretending to work on a script, I'm really watching Rain, who has just shown up, and she's tan and pacing the floor, holding a glass of ice with some tequila in it, chatting casually about how crazy her mother is and her younger stepbrother who's in the military and when she falls onto the lounge chair in the corner of the office it takes all the strength I have to get up and walk over to her and not say anything about Julian. She looks up at me and keeps talking, only lightly distracted, but when I don't answer a question she touches her knee against mine and then I reach for her arm and pull her off the chair and when she reminds me about the reservation at Dan Tana's I tell her, "I want to fuck you first," and start pulling her toward the bedroom.

"Come on," she says. "I'm hungry. Let's go to Dan Tana's."

"I thought you didn't want to go to Dan Tana's," I say, pressing into her. "I thought you wanted to go someplace else."

"I changed my mind."

"Why? Who didn't you want to see there?"

"Can't we just hang?"

"No," I say.

"Look," she says. "Maybe after dinner? I just want to chill." She strokes my face and then kisses me lightly on the lips and then she pulls her arm away and walks out of the office. I follow her through the living room and into the kitchen, where she heads for the tequila bottle and does another shot.

"Who was in San Diego?" I ask.

"What?"

"Who was in San Diego?" I ask again.

"My mother. I told you that about a hundred times."

"Who else?"

"Stop it, Crazy," she says. "Hey, did you talk to Jon and Mark?"

"Maybe."

"*Maybe?*" She makes a face. "What does that mean?"

I shrug. "It means maybe."

"Don't do that," she says quickly, whirling toward me. "Do not do that."

"Do what?"

"Threaten me," she says, before her face relaxes into a smile.

At Dan Tana's we're seated in the front room next to a booth of young actors and Rain tries to engage me, her foot rubbing against my ankle, and after a few drinks I mellow into acceptance even though a guy at the bar keeps glancing at Rain and for some reason I keep thinking he's the guy I saw her with in the parking lot at Bristol Farms, his arm in a sling, and then I realize I passed him on the bridge at the Hotel Bel-Air when I went to see Blair, and Rain's talking about the best way to approach the producer and director of *The Listeners* in terms of hiring her and how we need to do this carefully and that it's "superimportant" she gets the part because so much is riding on this for her and I'm zoning out on other things but I keep glancing back at the guy leaning against the bar and he's with a friend and they both look like they stepped out of a soap opera and then I suddenly have to interrupt her.

"There's no one else you're seeing, right?"

Rain stops talking, considers the vibe and asks, "Is that what this is about?"

"I mean, it's just me right now, right?" I ask. "I mean, whatever it is we're doing, you're not hanging out with another guy, right?"

"What are you talking about?" she asks. "Crazy, what are you doing?"

"When's the last time you had sex?"

"With you." She sighs. "Here we go." She sighs again. "What about you?"

"Do you care?"

"Look, I had a stressful week—"

"Stop it," I say. "You got a tan."

"Do you want to say something to me?" she asks.

I look around the room and she relents.

"I'm here with you now," she says. "Stop being such a girl."

I sigh and say nothing.

"What happened? Why are you so angry?" she asks after I order another drink. "I was only gone five days."

"I'm not angry," I say. "I just didn't hear from you . . ."

"Look." She scrolls through the iPhone I bought her and shows me pictures of herself with an older woman, the Pacific in the background.

"Who took these pictures?" I automatically ask.

"A friend of mine," she says. "A *girl*friend," she stresses.

"Why does that guy at the bar keep looking at you?"

Rain doesn't even glance at the bar when she says, "I don't know," and then shows me more pictures of herself in San Diego with the older woman I don't believe is her mother.

Heading up Doheny I'm looking through the windshield of the BMW and I notice the lights in the condo are on. Rain sits in the passenger seat, arms crossed, considering something.

"Did I leave the lights on?" I ask.

"No," she says, distracted. "I don't remember."

I make a right on Elevado to see if the blue Jeep is there and I cruise by the spot where it's usually parked and it isn't there, and after circling the block a couple of times I pull into the driveway of the Doheny Plaza and the valet takes the car and then Rain and I go back to 1508 and she lets me go down on her and when I'm hard enough she sucks me off, and when I wake up the next morning, she's gone.

Rain is the only topic discussed in Dr. Woolf's office on Sawtelle and I had referred to her anonymously in the last session while she was in San Diego as "this girl" but now with the information I have about Julian I tell him everything: how I had met Rain Turner at a Christmas party, and I realize while I'm describing that moment to Dr. Woolf that I had drinks with Julian at the Beverly Hills Hotel almost immediately afterward, and how I ran into her again at the casting sessions and then at the lounge on La Cienega, and I detail the days we spent together that last week of December and how I began to think it was real, like what I had with Meghan Reynolds, and then found out from Blair that Rain is supposedly Julian's girlfriend—at this point Dr. Woolf puts down his notepad and seems more patient with me than he probably is, and I'm trying to figure out the game plan and then realize Julian must have known that Rain and I had spent those days together but how was that possible? Finally, near the end of the session, Dr. Woolf says, "I would urge you not to see this girl anymore," and then "I would urge you to cut off all contact." After another long silence he asks, "Why are you crying?"

I'm not taking no for an answer," Rip says lightly, in singsong, over the phone after telling me to meet him at the observatory at the top of Griffith Park even though I'm hungover enough to forget how to fill the BMW's gas tank at the Mobil station on the corner of Holloway and La Cienega, and cutting across Fountain to avoid the traffic backed up on Sunset I call Rain three times, so distracted that she's not picking up I almost make a right onto Orange Grove in case she's there, but I can't deal. In the mostly deserted parking lot in front of the observatory Rip is on his phone, leaning against a black limousine, the driver listening to an iPod, the Hollywood sign gleaming in the background behind them. Rip is dressed simply in jeans, a green T-shirt, sandals. "Let's take a walk," Rip says, and then we're wandering across the lawn toward the dome of the planetarium, and on the West Terrace we're so high above the city it's soundless and the blinding sun reflected in the faraway Pacific makes it look as if the ocean's on fire, and the empty sky is completely clear except for the haze hanging over downtown where a dirigible floats above the distant skyscrapers and if I hadn't been so hungover the view would have been humbling.

"I like it up here," Rip says. "It's peaceful."

"It's a little out of the way."

"Yeah, but there's no one here," he says. "It's quiet up here. No one can follow you. We can talk without worrying about it."

"Worrying about what?"

Rip considers this. "That our privacy might be compromised." He pauses. "I'm like you: I don't trust people."

The sun is so bright it bleaches the terrace, and my skin begins to burn and the silence that drowns everything out makes even the most innocent figures in the distance seem filled with ominous intent as they roam slowly, cautiously, as if any natural movement would disrupt the stillness and we pass a Hispanic couple leaning against a ledge as we move across the Parapet Promenade and once we're on the walkway and moving toward the East Terrace, Rip softly asks me, "Have you seen Julian lately?"

"No," I say. "The last time I saw Julian was before Christmas."

"Interesting," Rip says, and then admits, "Well, I didn't think you had."

"Then why did you ask?"

"Just wanted to know how you'd answer that question."

"Rip—"

"There was a girl . . ." He stops, considers. "There's always a girl, isn't there?"

I shrug. "Yeah, I guess."

"Anyway, there was a girl I met about four or five months ago, and this girl worked for a very exclusive, superdiscreet . . . service." Rip pauses as two teenage boys speaking French pass by, and then looks around to see if anyone else is near us before he continues. "You can't find it on the Net, it's just word-of-mouth referrals so there's no, um, *viral* trail. Everything was handled among people who knew each other so it was all fairly contained."

"What . . . was the service?" I ask.

Rip shrugs. "Just really beautiful girls, really beautiful boys, kids who came out here to make it and needed cash and wanted to make sure that if they ever became Brad Pitt there's no hard evidence that they were involved in anything like this." Rip sighs, looks at the city and then back at me. "Comparatively expensive, but you're paying for the low-key and the no records and how totally anonymous it is."

"How did you find out about it?" I don't want to know the answer but the silence, amplified, ramped up, makes me ask just to say something.

"Well, that's one of the interesting parts of this story," Rip says. "The guy who started the service is someone we know. I guess you could say he's the one who hooked me up with the girl."

"Who are we talking about?" I ask, even though something tells me that I already know.

"Julian," Rip says, confirming it. "Julian ran it." Rip pauses. "I'm surprised you didn't know this already."

"Julian ran what, exactly?" I manage to ask.

"The service," Rip says. "He actually started it. All by himself. He's personable in that way. He knows a lot of kids. He brought them in." Rip thinks about it. "It's something he knows how to do." Another pause. "Julian's good at it."

"Why are you telling me this?" I ask. "I'm not interested in using an escort service to hook up and I'm definitely not interested in anything that has to do with Julian."

"Oh, that's a lie," Rip says. "That's a big lie."

"Why is that a lie?"

"Because Julian is how I met a girl named Rain Turner."

"I don't know who that is."

Rip parodies a brief scowl and makes a dismissive gesture with his hand. "Oh, dude, you handled that so awkwardly." He sighs, impatient. "That girl you've been hanging with? The so-called actress you promised to give a part to in your little movie? Does this ring a bell? Please, don't be an idiot with me."

I can't say anything. I'm suddenly gripping the iron railing. The information is an excuse not to look at him anymore. The fear, the big black stain of it, is rushing forward and it's in the heat and the vast expanse of empty terrace and everywhere else.

"You're shaking there, bro," Rip says. "Maybe you want to sit down?"

O n the East Terrace I'm finally numb enough to listen as Rip starts speaking again, after he takes a brief call confirming lunch and texts someone else back and we're sitting on a bench in direct sunlight and I feel my skin blistering and I can't move and up close Rip's face is androgynous and his eyelashes are tinted.

"Anyway, so I meet her and I like her and I think we hit it off and then I'm not paying for it anymore and I'm actually thinking about divorcing my wife, which shows you how committed I am to this girl." Rip keeps gesturing with his hands. "I tell Rain to quit the gig and she does. I take care of everything—pay the rent for her and the bitch roommate in that dump on Orange Grove, clothes, fucking hair, the Beamer, personal trainer, tanning salon, whatever she wants. I even got her a gig at that place on La Cienega, Reveal, all these things that Julian can't afford to do—and guess what she still really wants?"

Rip waits. I'm processing everything. And then it hits me and I say in a low voice, "She still wants to be an actress."

"Well, she wants to be famous," Rip says. "But at least you're paying attention," he says. "That's basically the correct answer."

I can't unclench my fists and Rip gets up and starts pacing in front of me.

"I think you know by now it's never going to happen for her, but anyway Julian's been bragging about what a great friend Clay is and that he'll be sure to hook her up with you and this movie that I guess you have some hand in casting. Whatever. I mean, it sounded like bullshit to me but you've gotta have hope, right?" Rip suddenly stops and checks his phone, then puts it back in his pocket. "But when you first got into town Julian kind of riled you up about something and I guess you guys didn't exactly hit it off that night so he didn't ask you to help out." Rip sighs, as if tired of it all, yet continues. "Somehow she manages to get an audition—something I admittedly don't really care about or have the juice to do and anyway I think it's a waste of time because she has no talent—and so she comes in and reads for you guys and I'm guessing she's just fuck-awful but she has her charms and the rest is . . . well, why don't you tell me what the rest is, Clay?"

I'm just sitting silently on the stone bench.

"I take it you've been banging her for a couple of weeks now?"

I don't say anything.

Rip sighs. "That's an answer in a way."

"Rip, please—"

"And then she splits for San Diego," Rip says. "Right?"

"She went to see her family."

"Family?" Rip scowls. "Did you know that Julian was in San Diego with her?"

"Why would I know that?" I say.

"Oh, come on, Clay—"

"Rip, please, what do you want?"

He considers this. "I want *her.*" And then he considers something else. "I mean, I know, I know, she's just a dumb cunt actress, right?"

I'm nodding and Rip registers the nods and cocks his head, curious.

"If you're agreeing with me, then why are you so beat up over her?" he asks.

"I don't know," I say quietly. "I just am."

"Have you ever thought that maybe this—your little freak-out—isn't about her?" Rip says. "That maybe it's about you?"

"No." I swallow. "I haven't."

"Look, you're not the threat," Rip says. "She's just using you. However . . . she really likes him." Rip pauses. "Julian's the problem."

"The problem? What are you talking about? Why is *he* the problem?"

"Julian is the problem," Rip says, "because Rain denied anything was going on with him until I found out about their little vacation in San Diego last week."

"She told me she went to see her mother," I say. "She showed me pictures of herself with her mother."

Rip fake-smiles. "So, she has a mother now? In San Diego? Sweet." But after he studies my reaction the smile fades.

"The first time I found out they were together I had gotten some information she couldn't lie her way out of and I let it go because she promised me she wouldn't go back to him or do anything with him but . . . this time . . . I just don't know."

"What don't you know?"

"This time . . . I don't know if I'll hurt him or not." Rip says this so gently and with so little menace that it doesn't sound like a threat and I start laughing.

"I'm serious," Rip says. "This is not a joke, Clay."

"I think that's a little extreme."

"That's because you're probably very sensitive."

After a long pause, Rip says flatly, "I only want one thing. I want her back."

"But obviously she wants someone else."

Rip takes a moment to study me. "You're a very bitter dude."

I'm leaning forward, clutching my sides. I glance at him before nodding.

"Yeah. I guess I am."

We're walking across the grass toward the black limo and the driver waiting there and Rip glances at the Astronomers Monument as we pass it and I'm staring straight ahead, unable to focus on anything but the heat and the surreal blue sky and the hawks sailing over the soundless landscape, their shadows crossing the lawn, and I wonder if I'm going to be able to make it back to Doheny without getting into an accident and then Rip asks me something that should have been just a formality but because of our conversation now isn't. "What are you doing the rest of the afternoon?"

"I don't know," I say, and then remember. "Are you going to Kelly's memorial?"

"That's today?"

"Yeah."

"No," Rip says. "Didn't really know him. We did some business, but that was a long time ago." The driver opens the door. "I've got to deal with this dickhead about the club. You know, the usual." He says this as if I should be hip enough to understand what exactly he means, and before getting into the limo Rip asks me, "When are you seeing her next?"

"I think maybe tonight." Then I can't help it and ask, "How do you feel about that?"

"Hey, I hope she gets the part. I'm rooting for her." He pauses, and grins. "Aren't you?"

I don't say anything. I just barely shake my head.

"Yeah," Rip says, convinced of something. "I thought so." And then, as he slides into the back of the limo and before the driver shuts the door, Rip looks up at me and says, "You have a history of this, don't you?"

I'm supposed to go to a Golden Globes party at the Sunset Tower tonight but Rain doesn't want to even after I tell her that Mark and Jon are going to be there and that if she wants the part of Martina I should formally introduce her to them outside of Jason's office in Culver City. "This isn't the way to do it," she mutters. "But it's the way we're going to do it," I tell her. When she arrives at my place, newly bronzed, her hair blown out, she's wearing a strapless dress, but I'm still in a robe, drinking vodka, stroking myself. She doesn't want to have sex. I turn away and tell her I'm not going if we don't. She downs two shots of Patrón in the kitchen and then strides into the bedroom and carefully takes off her dress and says, "Just don't kiss me," gesturing at her makeup and while I'm eating her out my fingers move to her ass and she brushes them away and says, "I don't want to do it like that." Later, as she's putting the dress back on, I notice a bruise on the side of her torso that I hadn't seen before. "Who did that to you?" I ask. She cranes her neck to look at the bruise. "Oh, that?" she says. "You did."

Entering the party at the Sunset Tower we're behind a famous actor and the cameras start flashing like a strobe and I pull Rain with me toward the bar and when I catch my reflection in a mirror my face is a skull, sunburned from the hour spent at the observatory, and on the terrace overlooking the pool, snaking through the hum of the crowd with Rain, I say hello to a few people I recognize while nodding to others I don't but who seem to recognize me and I make small talk with various people about the Kelly Montrose memorial even though I wasn't there and then I spot Trent and Blair and I move in another direction since I don't want

Blair to see me with Rain, and projected onto the walls are black-and-white photos of palm trees, stills of Palisades Park from the 1940s, girls who were cast in the new James Bond movie, and trays of doughnuts are being passed around and I'm chewing gum so I won't smoke and then I spot Mark with his wife and I bring Rain over to where they're standing and Mark frowns when he sees her, and then erases it with a smile before we fake-hug, his eyes never leaving Rain, his wife's reaction a barely concealed hostility, and then I launch into an explanation as to why I haven't been at the casting sessions and Mark says that I should come in tomorrow and I assure him I will and just as I'm about to make a pitch for Rain my phone vibrates in my pocket and I pull it out and there's a text from a blocked number that says *She knows* and after I type in *?* Mark and his wife drift off and Rain, seemingly uncaring that I didn't pitch her to Mark, is behind me talking to another young actress and a new text arrives: *She knows that you know.*

Heading back to the Doheny Plaza trying to keep steady on Sunset, I ask casually, "Do you know a guy named Julian Wells?" After I ask this I'm able to loosen my grip on the steering wheel—the question is a release.

"Hey, yeah," Rain says brightly, fooling with the stereo. "Do you know Julian?"

"Yeah," I say. "We grew up together out here."

"I didn't know that. Cool." She tries to find a track on a CD Meghan Reynolds had burned for me last summer. "He might have mentioned something about that."

"How do you know him?" I ask.

"I did some work for him," she says. "A long time ago."

"What kind of work?"

"Just like an assistant. Freelance," she says. "It was a long time ago."

"I actually know that you know him," I say.

"What's that supposed to mean?" she asks, concentrating on locating the song. "You say that so weird."

"Where is he right now?" I ask. "I'm just wondering."

"How would I know that?" she asks, pretending to be annoyed.

"Well, aren't you his girlfriend?"

Everything is suddenly in slow motion. It's as if suddenly she forgot her lines. Her only response is to laugh. "You're crazy."

"Let's call him up."

"Okay. Sure. Whatever, Crazy."

"You don't believe me, do you?" I say. "You think this is a joke?"

"I think you're crazy," she says. "That's what I think this is."

"I know about you and him, Rain."

"And what do you *think* you know?" Her voice remains playful.

"I know you were in San Diego with Julian last week."

"I was with my mother, Clay."

"But you were also with Julian." Saying this relaxes me. "Didn't you think I was going to find out about this?"

At the light on Doheny she stares straight out the windshield.

"Didn't you know I was going to find out that you're still fucking him?"

She suddenly cracks. She whirls toward me in the passenger seat. A series of questions pour out in a pleading rush. "So what? What does it matter? What are you doing? What do you think this is about? Will you just leave it alone? What does it matter what I do when I'm not with you?"

"It matters," I say. "In this situation, for you to get what you want, it matters very much."

"Why does it matter?" she shouts. "You're crazy."

I calmly make the left and start heading down Doheny.

"You couldn't even play this part for a fucking month?" I ask quietly. "What, you needed his cock so badly that you had to jeopardize everything for yourself? If being with me was so important to you, Rain, why did you fuck it up? You could've played me but—"

"I don't *play* people, Clay."

"What about Rip Millar?"

"What about Rip Millar?" she says. "Jesus, you need to get over yourself."

The blurry headlights from oncoming cars cause me to pull the BMW to the side of the road across from the Doheny Plaza.

"Get out. Just get out of the fucking car."

"Clay . . ." She reaches for me. "Please, stop."

"You're panicking." I smile, pulling away from her. "Look at this: you're really panicking."

"Listen, I'll do whatever you want," she says. "What do you want? Just tell me what you want and I'll do it."

"End things with Julian now," I say. "At least until you get the part."

She pulls back. "How do I even know that you'll help me get the part?"

"I will," I say. "But just tell Julian to go away. I'm not even going to try until he's out of the picture."

"If you get me the part I'll do anything," she says quietly. "I'll do anything you want. If you can get me that part I'll do anything you want."

She grabs my face. She pulls me to her. She kisses me hard on the mouth.

In the darkness of the bedroom Rain asks me, "Why did you do this now?"

"Do what?" I'm propped on a pillow sipping vodka and melted ice.

"Bring this all up," she says. "Try and wreck everything."

"I just wanted to prove that you were lying to me."

"Who told you?"

"Rip Millar."

She immediately tightens up and her voice becomes chilled.

"That's not happening anymore."

"Why isn't it happening?"

"Because he's fucked up." She turns to me. "Don't bring Rip into this. Please, Clay? Seriously. Just don't. I'll handle Rip."

"He said he'll hurt Julian," I say. "He said he won't be able to help himself."

"Why can't you just let this be what it is?"

"Because what it is . . . is not what I want."

"If this is going to work the way you want it to"—she sighs—"I need some money."

"You have a job," I say. "What about Reveal?"

"I was let go," she says finally.

"Why?"

"Rip made a call," she says. "He hates me."

Things start expanding. I feel more relaxed. Everything becomes possible because the plan starts falling into place.

"Did you hear me?" she asks.

"How do you live like this?"

"I pretend I don't."

Is she with you now? Where is she, Julian? I mean, I know what's going on. I know what the facts are. Fuck, Julian, what are you fucking doing? Are you fucking with me again? You're pimping your girlfriend out? What kind of fucked-up dude are you? Tell me where she is . . . Where is she? . . . Oh, fuck yourself. I don't ever want to see your fucking face ever again and if I see you I swear to God I will fucking kill you, Julian. I mean it. I'll fucking kill you and I won't give a shit. I'll like it because everything will be better once you're dead." A drunken message I leave on Julian's cell phone when I wake up and Rain's gone in the middle of a warm January night, after the Golden Globes party at the Sunset Tower.

Two catering trucks are parked in front of the casting complex in Culver City and in the courtyard a crew is setting up tables and a DJ stand and the patio is filled with waiting young actors dressed in vintage eighties clothes and they all have blond bangs and then I'm passing the pool and walking up the stairs into an office where Jon and Mark are taking a break from the auditions with Jason.

"He's back from the dead," Jon says. "What's up? Where have you been?"

"Just some personal stuff I had to deal with," I say. "I had to finish a script." I put my hands in my pockets and lean against a wall, trying to remain loose and casual. "And I've been thinking that we saw someone who's perfect for Martina."

"We still haven't found anyone yet," Jon says.

"Well, that's not true," Jason says. "We've narrowed it down but who are you thinking of?"

Mark is just staring at me, slightly amused, maybe bewildered. "Yeah, who is it?" He asks this as if he already knows.

"We saw her a couple of weeks ago and, well, I've been thinking about her a lot," I say. "I think we should see her again."

"Who?"

"Rain Turner. Do you remember her?" I ask, then turn to Mark. "She was with me at the party last night."

Jason swings over to his monitor and taps some keys and Rain's headshot appears on the screen. Jon moves forward, confused. Mark glances at the screen and then, hope-lessly, at me.

"Why her?" Jon asks. "She's older than Martina."

"She just seems like who I had in mind when I was writing the script," I say. "I mean, Martina could be a few years older than the others."

"She's very pretty," Jon murmurs. "But I don't really remember who she was."

"I think she's too old," Jason says.

"Why are you so sure about her, Clay?" Mark asks.

"I just can't stop thinking about her in that role and, well, I'd really like to have her read again."

"Has she become a friend of yours?" Mark asks.

I try to ignore the way he asks this. "No, I mean no . . . she's, I mean, I know her."

"Who is this girl?" Jon asks. "Who reps her?"

"Burroughs Media," the casting director says reading from the screen. "ICM is listed but I don't think they're repping her anymore. Her last credits are from a year ago." He keeps scanning and then stops. "Actually, she got in as a favor."

"From who?" I'm the one who asks this.

The casting director scrolls down Rain's page. There's a sudden hesitancy in the room before Jason says anything.

"Kelly Montrose," he says. "Kelly made the call."

Everything goes silent. Things become reversed in the long moment before anyone says anything. Through the open window the palm tree waves in the dry wind and the kids are murmuring below by the pool and no one in the room knows what to say and the hangover I had forgotten about returns the moment Kelly Montrose's name is men-tioned and I want to sing softly to myself to help submerge the pain—the chest that aches, the blood pulsing in my head—and I have no choice except to pretend I'm only a phantom, neutral and uncaring.

"Well, that's not good," Jon says. "I think that's a bad omen."

"Yeah?" I ask, finding my voice. "You do?"

"I'm superstitious." Jon shrugs. "I believe in bad luck."

"When did this happen?" I ask Jason. "When did Kelly make the call for her?"

"A couple days before he disappeared," Jason says.

Rain calls me after I text her *Kelly Montrose?*

"Where did you go last night?" I ask. "Why did you leave? Were you with Julian?"

"If this is going to work the way you want it to," she says, "I have to take care of some things first."

"What things?" I'm walking out of the complex, holding the phone tightly against my ear.

"You can't ask me that."

"I talked to them about you." I realize I'm unable to move while I'm on the phone with her. "They're going to see you again."

"Thanks," she says. "But listen, I have to go."

"There's a party tonight," I say. "Here in Culver City."

"I don't think I can make that, Clay."

"Rain—"

"Just give me a day or two and then we can be together, okay?"

"Why didn't you tell me you knew Kelly Montrose?"

"I'll explain everything when I see you," she says. "I have to go."

"Why didn't you tell me Kelly Montrose got you the audition?" I'm whispering this.

"You never asked," she says, and then hangs up.

There's nothing to do but wait for the party and since I have nowhere else to go I stick around Culver City, skipping the afternoon auditions, the fear returning as I walk to a liquor store to buy aspirin, the alcoholic dreaminess of everything, the ghosts swarming everywhere whispering *You need to be careful who you let into your life,* and I'm pacing the courtyard while I return a couple of calls—leaving messages for the agent, the manager, the movie about the monkeys, Dr. Woolf—and smoking cigarettes by the swimming pool and watching the decorating crew string up lights along the length of a curving beige wall that borders one end of the pool and then I'm introduced to the actor who got the main role of Grant, Kevin Spacey's son, in *The Listeners* and the boy is unusually handsome even with the beard he has because of the pirate movie he's shooting and screens have been set up and headshots of various young actors are flashing on them and then from somewhere complaints are made and the screens are repositioned and I meet another girl who won another modeling competition and the afternoon becomes grayer, the sky shrouded with clouds, and someone asks me, "What's the matter, dude?"

The party surrounds the pool and paper lanterns are strung along the courtyard and songs from the eighties are playing and everyone's familiar-looking even though they're all eighteen and I'm hoping that Rain will surprise me by showing up but also knowing that she won't. Cade, the trainer from Equinox, is here—I forgot that I had made the call—and now that I understand what his connection to Julian really is I'm embarrassed Cade thinks I'm clueless enough not to know, and I'm standing next to one of Jason's assistants and drinking vodka from a plastic cup and the boy playing Kevin Spacey's son keeps asking me questions about his character that I answer in a monotone and he responds by pointing out an owl that's nesting in the palm tree and then I see the actress—she's a girl, really—that I hit on in the first-class lounge at JFK before Christmas, maybe a month ago, and Amanda Flew is so much younger than I remember and whenever she glances over at me she smiles nervously at the boy she's talking to and sometimes the boy whispers in her ear and another boy lights her cigarettes and I'm now aware that I've drunk too much.

"Do you know that girl?" I ask the assistant. "Amanda Flew?"

"Yeah," the assistant says. "Do you know her?"

"Yeah," I say. "I fucked her."

There's a beat but when I look over at him he says, "Cool." He shrugs but he's creeped out. "She's hot. She's slammin'." Another pause. "I guess she likes older guys, huh?"

"Yeah, I guess." I shrug too, and then ask, "Why do you say that?"

"I thought she was one of Rip Millar's girls."

I'm watching as Amanda gets a text, glances at it and then makes a call. She barely says anything, just listens, and then clicks off.

"His girls?" I'm asking.

"Yeah," the assistant says and then noting my reaction in just those two words, adds, "I mean, it's not like a secret or anything. She was part of his pussy posse." He pauses. "But I've heard she's crazy. Really messed up."

I don't say anything.

"But maybe that's how you like them," the assistant says.

When Amanda sees me approaching she turns away as if I'm not there. She looks around the party, she blinks, she doesn't say anything, but when I intimately push myself into her group it becomes awkward for her to ignore me and then I say "Hey" and her smile is there and then it isn't. She seems upset that I'm standing next to her, that I've even approached her, and I realize that after being so flirtatious in the lounge at JFK she now doesn't want to speak to me but I just stand there, hoping she'll say something back and behind Amanda a girl is dancing by herself to an old Altered Images song, the tattoo of a phone number inked along her arm.

"Yeah?" Amanda says. "Hi." Then she turns back to the two guys.

"We met in New York," I say. "At JFK. I think you texted me a couple of times since you've been in L.A. but we haven't spoken in like four weeks. How are you?"

"I'm fine," she says, and then there's an awkward silence and the two guys introduce themselves and names are exchanged and one of them recognizes me and says "Oh, cool" and then turns his attention on me but I'm focusing on Amanda.

"Yeah, it's been around a month," I say, staring at her. "You doing okay?"

"I'm fine, I said," and then, "But I think maybe you've made a mistake."

"Aren't you up for a role in *The Listeners*?"

A photographer snaps a shot of us standing together and it's either this or the question I asked that becomes Amanda's cue to leave. "I have to go now."

I start trailing after her. "Hey, wait a minute."

"I can't talk right now," she says.

"Hey, I said wait a minute—"

She's backed against a wall that leads to the exit. The conversation is on the verge of becoming an argument.

"You're being rude," she says.

"I haven't done anything," I say. "Why am I making you so uncomfortable?"

For one flashing second her eyes go wild and then she relents.

"Please don't talk to me, okay?" She tries to smile. "I don't even know you," she says. "I don't even know who you are."

It's raining lightly when I leave the party and I forget where the BMW is and then I finally find it parked against a curb a few blocks away on Washington Boulevard and as I'm about to pull out a blue Jeep rushes by and slows to a stop at the light behind me on the corner. I make a U-turn and pull up behind the Jeep and my hair is wet and my hands are shaking and I can't see who's inside the car and it starts to rain harder as I follow the Jeep up Robertson toward West Hollywood and through the windshield wipers the streets seem emptier because of the rain and on the CD Meghan Reynolds burned for me last summer Bat for Lashes is singing "What's a Girl to Do?" and lightning illuminates a turquoise mural on a freeway underpass and then the Jeep makes a right on Beverly and I keep checking the rearview mirror to see if someone's following me but I can't tell and then I force myself to stop weeping and turn off the stereo concentrating only on the blue Jeep as it makes a left onto Fairfax, and then I'm sobering up completely as the Jeep turns right onto Fountain and then a sharp right onto Orange Grove and a left about half a block up from Santa Monica Boulevard into the driveway adjacent to Rain's apartment. And then Amanda Flew gets out of the blue Jeep.

I cruise by the apartment and turn in to a driveway down the street and park illegally, letting the engine run, and I don't know what to do—every logical thought has become eclipsed—but I manage to get out of the BMW and move across the front lawn toward the building and it keeps raining but I don't care, and Rain's apartment is on the ground floor of the two-story complex and all the lights in the apartment are on and Rain's pacing the living room, on the phone, smoking a cigarette, and I stand away from the window out of the light and Rain's wearing a robe and her face is swollen and wiped clear of makeup and the beauty of it is momentarily blurred and despite the panic infusing the apartment candles have still been lit and I can't hear anything except for a door slamming and then Rain clicks off the phone and Amanda walks in and I can't hear what they're saying to each other even when Rain starts shouting at her. Amanda says something that makes Rain stop shouting and she listens to Amanda and then both girls suddenly become hysterical and when Amanda reaches out, clutching at her, Rain slaps Amanda across the face. Amanda tries to slap Rain back but then she falls into Rain's arms and they hold each other for a long time until Amanda sinks to her knees. Rain leaves her there and hurriedly packs a gym bag that's sitting on the couch and Amanda, frantic, crawls toward Rain and tries to stop her. Rain throws the gym bag at Amanda, and Amanda clutches at it, weeping. And when I realize that Amanda Flew is Rain's roommate I have to look away.

Two silent flashes behind me briefly illuminate the side of the building and when I turn around that's when I notice a black Mercedes double-parked on Orange Grove, the flashes coming from the open window on the passenger side, and then the window rolls up. A vague realization: someone was taking pictures of me standing in front of Rain and Amanda's apartment. Shaking, I ignore the car and slowly move away from the apartment and walk down the street to the idling BMW. I get in. I pull away from the curb. I roll up Orange Grove past the Mercedes, which then starts following me as I pull up to Fountain and make a left. So does the black car. I gun the BMW forward but in the rearview mirror the Mercedes keeps up, veering in and out of lanes. I floor the accelerator in order to make the light and swerve onto La Cienega. The Mercedes makes the light too, its tires screeching against the wet asphalt. I stop at the light on Holloway, the high beams of the black car pressing against the BMW, and then take a right on Santa Monica, trying to act casual, as if I'm suddenly unaware of the Mercedes. But it follows me back to the Doheny Plaza and when I valet the BMW I pretend not to see the Mercedes as it cruises around the corner onto Norma Place, slowing as I turn and walk into the lobby, and I only hear it speed away.

In the condo, shaking and wet, holding a glass of vodka with both hands in the darkness of the balcony, storms sweeping over the city, I'm watching the black Mercedes cruise back and forth on Elevado and then I get a text from a blocked number—*Hey gringo, you can't hide*—accompanied by a winking smiley face, and that night I dream about the boy, the same dream that Rain had but now the boy, beautiful and shirtless, has moved from the kitchen into the living room and I keep asking him, "Who are you?" and for some reason he's gesturing at me, the muscles in his arms and chest straining, and as he moves closer I can see the tattoo of a dragon on his forearm and there's blood in the boy's hair and when I stumble into the guest bathroom in the middle of the night, scattering a few of Rain's things that line the sink, I turn on the lights, and in the mirror above the counter, written in something red, are two words: DISAPPEAR HERE.

Another awards party, this one at Spago, and though there's always the risk of seeing someone you don't want to I'm beyond caring and since Rain isn't coming over until tomorrow I find myself standing in the main dining room accidentally stuck in a conversation with Muriel and Kim who don't ask me why I wasn't at the party for Alana at Blair's and after a photographer takes a picture of the three of us they move away, and it's okay that Trent and Blair are in the courtyard because neither one of them will talk to me since there are too many people at the party tonight. Daniel Carter keeps smiling impatiently at me and though I don't want Daniel to come over, Meghan Reynolds doesn't seem to be around and there's nothing to do but stand still and Daniel and I are both wearing James Perse T-shirts and expensive one-button blazers and he asks about *The Listeners* and I tell him that I liked his movie, that I was at the premiere in December, and then we're talking about how big the new *Friday the 13th* opened and discussing how a particular special effect was accomplished while Daniel keeps craning his neck, raising his eyebrows at someone across the room and smiling.

"Looks like you got some sun there," Daniel says, gesturing at my reddened face.

"Yeah," I say. "You know me: I get burned easily."

"You've been in New York, right?" Daniel asks. "How long are you here? I heard you were back at Doheny."

"I don't know how long I'm back," I say. "New York seems . . . over."

"And this place is . . . ?" Daniel asks, waiting for me to complete the sentence.

"Happening." I shrug. "I'm a different person now." I put on a fake smile.

"Please don't tell me you're thinking of moving back," he says. "Fuck, if I could get out of here . . ."

And then Meghan comes up to us and leans slightly into Daniel and says "Hi, Clay" and if I weren't drunk I wouldn't have been able to stand being here and I had forgotten how Meghan looks close-up and it shocks me like it always did and I have to pretend nothing's wrong. Meghan gazes at me indifferently and my fake smile is a rebuke that lets her know I'm glad she's come to terms with all the things she'd done to me, and near the end of everything I had begged her to run away from this place and we were sitting at a sushi bar on Ventura Boulevard in Studio City and it was summer and I remember seeing a child actor who had been famous once and was now considered old at thirty-three, sitting at the far end of the sushi bar while Meghan kept hinting that it was over between us. Now, in Spago, I have no idea what Meghan has told Daniel about me even though she has a role in his next movie. She mentions she'd seen me at a screening I wasn't at, and I suddenly remember pacing outside the ER at Cedars-Sinai apologizing to her on the Fourth of July.

"Hey," Daniel says, "I'd like to talk to you about an idea." He mentions a script I wrote called *Adrenaline* that the studio had put into turnaround.

"Cool," I say. I'm holding a glass that's empty except for ice and limes, the remnants of a margarita.

"You're so thin," Daniel murmurs before he walks away with Meghan.

Rain has called twice and left a text and I've ignored them but when I see Daniel whispering something into Meghan's ear as they leave Spago I return Rain's call and she doesn't pick up.

Dr. Woolf leaves a message on my landline canceling tomorrow's session and telling me that he can't see me as a patient anymore but that he'll refer me to someone else and the next morning I drive to the building on Sawtelle and park on the fourth floor of the garage and wait for his noon session to be over because that's when he takes his lunch break and I'm listening to a song with the lyric *So leave everything you know and carry only what you fear* . . . over and over again and I'm nodding to myself while smoking cigarettes and making a list of all the things I'm not going to ask Rain about and deciding I'll accept all the false explanations she's going to give me and how that's the only plan, and then I'm remembering the person who warned me about how the world has to be a place where no one is interested in your questions and that if you're alone nothing bad can happen to you.

In the stillness of the garage Dr. Woolf unlocks a silver Porsche. I get out of my car and walk toward him and call out his name. He pretends not to hear me at first and then he's startled when he turns around. He's annoyed when he sees who it is, but then his face relaxes almost as if he'd been expecting this.

"Why can't you see me anymore?" I ask.

"Look, I'm just not able to help you—"

"But why?" I keep nearing him. "I don't get it."

"Have you been drinking?" he asks, pulling a cell phone out of his pocket like it's a warning of some kind.

"No, I haven't been drinking," I mutter.

"There's a very good guy in West Hollywood who I'll refer you to."

"I don't give a shit," I say. "I don't want a fucking referral."

"Clay, calm down—"

"Why the fuck are you dropping me as a patient?"

"Hey, Clay, between us . . ." He pauses, makes a pained gesture, and his voice softens. "Denise Tazzarek." He lets the name hang there in the shadows of the garage. "I'm not able to help you with . . . that."

I stand there for a second, wavering. "Wait, who's Denise Tazzarek?"

"The person you've been seeing," he says. "The one you talked about in the last session."

"What about her?"

He looks at me as if I shouldn't be confused.

"The girl you're talking about is a woman named Denise Tazzarek," he says, lowering his voice. "I know who she is."

"I don't understand."

"I know who this is and I'm not getting involved with her," he says. "I've had two patients involved with her and it's becoming a conflict of interest." He pauses. "There's nothing I can do."

"And you think this is . . . the same girl?"

"Yes," he says. "It's the same girl. Her real name is Denise Tazzarek," he says. "This girl you were talking about, Rain Turner? She's Denise Tazzarek."

I'm bracing myself again, insanely alert. "What do you know about her that . . . I don't know?"

"I told you in our last session: just stay away from her," he says, moving back to the Porsche. "That's all you really need to know."

I move closer to him. "So you know Rip Millar?"

"Clay—" He swings into the driver's seat.

"And Julian Wells?"

"I have to go—"

"What about Kelly Montrose?"

Dr. Woolf puts the key in the ignition but stops suddenly at the mention of that name. Turning back to me he looks up and says, "Kelly Montrose was a patient of mine." And then he closes the door and drives away.

The valet at the Doheny Plaza opens the door of the BMW for me and as I get out he says someone's waiting in the lobby and that's when I see Julian's Audi, streaked with mud and rain, parked in front of the building. Walking toward the lobby I almost turn around and get back into the BMW but a wave of anger makes a decision for me. Julian's wearing Ray-Bans and sitting in a chair casually checking his phone but I can still see the slightly swollen left eye and the split lip, and the faint black and purple bruises on his tan neck and the bandaged wrist. I don't say anything as I walk past him. I just make a gesture for him to get up and follow me. The doorman behind the desk glances at Julian worriedly and then at me before I say, "It's okay." Julian walks with me to the elevator and we don't say anything as he follows behind me down the hallway on the fifteenth floor and the only sound is when he clears his throat as I unlock the door and we step inside the apartment.

Julian carefully sits down on the sectional and he's stylishly dressed and seems okay despite what happened to him and he looks like he's making an attempt at keeping it together but he grimaces slightly when he places his foot on the ottoman and when he takes off the sunglasses with the hand whose wrist is bandaged the extent of the bruising is revealed.

"What happened to you?" I ask.

"Nothing," he says. "Doesn't matter."

"Who did that to you?"

"I don't know," Julian says, and then searching for an answer says something that sounds more like a suggestion. "Some Mexican kids." And then: "I'm not here to talk about that."

"Why are you here?"

"I know that you know about Rain," he says. "You didn't need to leave that message the other night. I think everyone knows what's going on."

"Jesus, Julian, what the fuck are you doing?" I ask in a hushed voice.

"It probably seems more complicated to you than it really is."

"That's because you made it more complicated."

He sighs, staring out the sliding glass doors at the afternoon light dimming over the city. "Can I have a glass of water?"

"It isn't complicated for me."

"Well, I guess I'm sorry, but it isn't all about you, Clay."

"What does that even mean?" I say, standing over him. "I don't even know what that means."

"It means that there's a larger world out there and it's not all about you."

"You're fucking crazy," I mutter. "You're all fucking crazy."

"It is what it is, Clay."

"Shut up," I mutter, pacing the floor, lighting a cigarette. "What is this bullshit—*it is what it is*?"

"I'm not sure why you're so pissed," Julian says. "You got what you wanted."

"And did you get what you wanted?" I gesture at the bruises. "Did Rip do this to you?"

"I told you," Julian says, "it was these Mexican kids." And then he asks again for some water.

When I bring Julian a bottle of Fiji, he nods thanks and says after taking a careful sip, "I don't talk to Rip anymore."

"Why not?" I ask. "Oh, wait, let me guess."

Julian shrugs and winces as he leans over and places the small plastic bottle on the ottoman. "It wasn't so much about me."

"Well, then what do you think it was about if it wasn't about you?"

"Rip snapped when Rain was with Kelly—"

"What does *snapped* mean?" I ask, cutting him off. "So your girlfriend was fucking Rip and then she's fucking Kelly? And you're still with her?"

"Clay, it's more complicated than—"

"Why is Kelly Montrose dead, Julian?" I ask, standing

over him, my hand holding the cigarette shaking. "What happened to Kelly? Why is he dead?"

Julian looks at me and realizes something. Still staring at me he debates whether to say anything. "Look, don't try and connect it all."

"Why not?"

"This isn't a script," Julian says. "It's not going to add up. Not everything's going to come together in the third act."

"What was Rip's connection to Kelly?"

"At first it was about Kelly investing in a club and they had a . . . falling-out."

"Over Rain?"

Julian shrugs. "That was part of it, I guess."

I try again: "I just want to know what I'm involved with. Just tell me."

"What *you're* involved with?" Julian seems surprised. "You're not involved in any of it. Maybe it feels like you are but you're not."

"Amanda Flew is Rain's roommate, right?"

"Yeah, she is," Julian says, confused. "Didn't you know that?"

"She drives a blue Jeep, right?" I say. "Why has she been following me?"

"She left town. Mandy's not here anymore," Julian says. "I don't know why she was following you." Pause. "Are you sure it was her?"

"And both of them were with Rip?" I ask. "Both Rain and Amanda had been with Rip?"

He sighs. "When Rain and I took a break Rip started hitting on her . . . and then, when she met Kelly, well, Rip started hanging out with Mandy," Julian says. "And that didn't last, and then he tried to get back with Rain but . . . that wasn't going to work."

"Why not?"

"Because he's . . . difficult." He pauses. "Or don't you know that by now?"

I lean into Julian, my voice lowered. "There are people staking out this apartment, Julian. There are cars on Elevado watching this place at night. There are people breaking in and going through my stuff. I get texts warning me about shit and I don't even know what shit they're warning me about but I think they're all connected to . . ." And suddenly I can't say it: *your girlfriend.* All I can say is "Don't lie to me. I know you're still together."

Julian slowly offers a small and noncommittal shrug. "Well, if you stop seeing her maybe the rest will stop." He considers something else. "If you don't want to see her anymore and you don't want to help her, then maybe all of that stuff will stop." He reaches for the water again. "Maybe this wasn't thought out enough. Maybe there were too many . . . I don't know . . . variables . . . that I didn't know about."

A long silence before I say, "You're leaving something out."

"What am I leaving out?" He seems genuinely curious.

"One of the variables."

"Which one?" He almost seems afraid to ask this.

"I like her."

Julian sighs and starts to sit up. "Clay—"

"And I don't really care what other shit is going down."

"Do you really like her, Clay?" Julian asks sadly. "Or do you like something else?"

"What does that mean, Julian?"

"You've been through this before," he says, carefully

choosing his words. "You know what this town is like. What did you expect? You barely know her. She's an actress."

"I'm listening to *you*? You're running an escort service and I'm listening to you?"

Julian sighs again. "I was just doing favors. It was small time. Come off it. Don't be so naïve."

"You're pimping your girlfriend out and you're telling me shit like that?"

"Okay, look, I can see where you're at. I can see where this is all going. I just wanted to say I'm sorry." He gets up and leans on the back of the sectional for support. "I should have known that you'd react this way. I thought you would have found it, I don't know, fun . . . that, y'know, you'd get something out of it and, well, she'd get something out of it and you wouldn't take it so seriously."

"That's why you were so interested in the movie, isn't it?" I say. "Because you wanted me to give your girlfriend a part?"

"Well, yeah." Julian pauses. "We thought it might work. But if you're not going to see her anymore we'll just call it quits."

"That might have to be adjusted."

"What do you mean?"

"Because I'm seeing her tonight," I say.

"I know you are," Julian says. "Because you're still going to help her, right?"

The last time Rain sees Amanda Flew is on the Sunday following the night when I stood outside of the apartment on

Orange Grove and, according to Rain, Amanda spends that night in her room and everything is "fine," though because of what I saw that night, I know everything was not "fine," and that something had happened that was pushing Amanda out of town. Amanda is supposed to leave the next day to stay with Mike and Kyle in Palm Springs and just "chill" for a couple of weeks but because she sleeps late and is scattered by the reasons she has to leave L.A. she doesn't get out of the apartment on Orange Grove until after dark. Rain never wanted Amanda—a girl she has now described to me as "too trusting"—to make this drive alone, and definitely not at night, and definitely not with twenty thousand dollars in cash in one of the gym bags she's carrying, but Amanda insists to the point where she's soon threatening not to go at all, so Rain and the two guys in Palm Springs tell Amanda that the only way this will work is if Amanda makes contact with them every ten minutes whether it's with Rain or with Mike and Kyle at the house in the desert, and Amanda agrees and leaves Orange Grove at 8:45 and doesn't call Rain until she's passing through downtown L.A. at 9:15. After this initial call things seem to fall apart fairly quickly.

From about 9:30 until 10:00 Amanda doesn't answer her phone. A call is made to the house in Palm Springs around 10:15 and Amanda sounds calm and tells Mike and Kyle that she's going to be later than she thought, that she's meeting someone at a coffee shop in Riverside but it's cool, and not to tell Rain. Apparently, neither Rain nor Mike nor Kyle thinks this is cool and Mike immediately starts driving to the coffee shop in Riverside. The next call to Kyle is at eleven and Amanda says she's not in Riverside anymore but has driven to Temecula. Kyle calls Mike and warns him that she's not in Riverside, and Amanda doesn't answer any of Rain's calls or texts—*This is totally fucked,* one of them reads, *you're going to die*—and an argument ensues about calling 911 and then is quickly dropped, and according to a waitress Mike talks to at the coffee shop in Riverside, Amanda had met two men at the entrance of the coffee shop and Amanda even kissed one of them on the cheek, though the waitress couldn't get a clear view of the one Amanda had kissed. The last call is made an hour later and Amanda is explaining to Kyle that she'll see him tomorrow, even after Kyle has warned her that Mike's leaving Riverside and on his way to Temecula. At this point someone takes the phone from Amanda and listens as Kyle starts shouting for Amanda to tell him exactly where she is, and Kyle can hear Amanda in the background whining, "Come on, stop it, give me back the phone, come on."

"Who is this? Hello?" Kyle shouts before the line goes dead.

Amanda never made it to Palm Springs the next morning and when it's confirmed to Rain that Amanda never showed up the following afternoon this is taken for some reason as a bad sign and not something someone who has been described to me as "crazy" and "really messed up" and who Rain slapped across the face in the apartment on

Orange Grove and who had read my palm in an airport
lounge and who had an affair with Rip Millar, who was, in
fact, a member of his "pussy posse," would be prone to do.
The first ominous news comes in early this evening: Mike
and Kyle find Amanda's blue Jeep in a parking lot off Inter-
state 10 outside of Indio. All of her bags are gone, including
the one with the twenty thousand dollars in cash.

I'm listening patiently as Rain tries to give me a version of
the story that's been edited carefully enough that I don't
have to ask any questions and she says she shouldn't be telling me this at all but the need is apparently overwhelming
even though she has erased the real fear of it as she tries to
keep it together with Patrón and a joint and assuring herself
that Amanda will show up eventually. I keep telling Rain
that maybe there was a mystery Amanda needed to solve. I
tell Rain that maybe Amanda wanted the answer to something. The other thing that soothes Rain, besides the tequila
and the dope and the Xanax I've given her, is the callback
for *The Listeners* that I arranged for next week.

"What does Julian think?" I ask when she's been silent
too long. "About Amanda?"

She can't answer that question because Julian's name
can't be mentioned between us anymore. I finish the drink
I'm holding.

"Well, maybe Rip's involved in this," I say, imitating a
child investigating a crime. "Isn't Rip fucking her too? He
must be very worried as well."

Rain just shrugs, ignoring me. "Maybe."

"Maybe he's worried or maybe he's fucking her or maybe he's involved in this?"

She says nothing, just stares out the window of my office, slumped on the chair while I sit behind my desk watching her.

"If you think her disappearance is connected to Rip shouldn't you go to the police?" I ask, my voice idle and detached.

Rain turns and looks at me like I'm insane.

"You don't care, do you?" she asks.

"You never told me what happened between you and Kelly Montrose."

"It was nothing. Whatever anyone told you, it's not true." She turns back to the drink and finishes it. "Nothing ever happened between me and Kelly."

"I don't believe you," I say, swiveling slowly back and forth in my chair, planning how this scene will play out. "You must have promised him something."

"Not everyone's like you."

I don't say anything.

"Maybe Kelly wanted something to happen," she finally admits. "Maybe that's why he made the call for me. I don't know."

"And maybe that explains why Rip got so angry," I say, trying to remain calm, trying to rein in my excitement. "Maybe he felt Kelly was about to make a move on you . . ."

"Rip Millar is just . . . very fucked up."

"Maybe that's why the two of you got along so well."

"Are you seriously talking to me like this?"

"You knew something that day," I tell her. "You knew that something had happened to Kelly. The day before you left for San Diego with that piece of shit. Kelly hadn't been found yet, but you knew that Rip had done something—"

"Fuck off," she screams.

"I don't really care anymore," I finally say, moving toward her, stroking her neck.

"You really don't care, do you?"

"I didn't know her, Rain."

"But you know me."

"No. I don't."

I lean in to kiss her face.

She turns away. "I don't want to," she mutters.

"Then get out of here," I say. "I don't care if you ever come back here."

"Amanda's missing and you're—"

"I said I don't care." I take her hand. I start pulling her toward the bedroom. "Come on."

"Just let it go, Clay." Her eyes are closed and she's grimacing.

"If you're not going to do this, then you should leave."

"And if I leave, what will happen?"

"I'll make a call to Mark. I'll make another call to Jon. I'll call Jason." I pause. "And I'll cancel everything."

She immediately moves into me and says she's sorry and then she's guiding me toward the bedroom and this is the way I always wanted the scene to play out and then it does and it has to because it doesn't really work for me unless it happens like this.

"You should be more compassionate," she says later, in the darkness of the bedroom.

"Why?" I ask. "Why should I be more compassionate?"

"You're a Pisces."

I pause, letting the statement hang there while it defines where I've ended up.

"How do you know that?"

"Amanda told me," she says quietly.

I don't say anything, even though it's hard to leave that statement alone.

"What's the worst thing that ever happened to you?" she asks, and it sounds like an echo. I know what it is but pretend that I don't.

At the Getty there's a dinner thrown by two Dream-Works executives for a curator of a new exhibit and I go alone and I'm in a better mood, just floating through it all, looking good, a little buzzed, and I'm standing on the terrace gazing out over the blackest sky and asking myself, What would Mara say? And on the tram ride up the hill I was in the same car as Trent and Blair and I was listening to Alana share her frustrations about a plastic surgeon and I nodded while watching the traffic speeding by on the 405 below us and from where I'm standing now nothing is visible in the darkened canyons until the lights of the hushed city fan out of that darkness and I keep checking my phone for messages and I'm almost done with my second martini when a boy in a catering uniform tells me that dinner will be served in fifteen minutes and then that boy is replaced by Blair.

"I hope you're not driving tonight," she says.

"Hey, I had a bad feeling when I showed up but I'm happy now."

"You look like you're in a good mood."

"I am."

"When I saw you at Spago the other night I didn't think you could possibly be happy."

"Well, I am now."

She pauses. "I don't think I want to know why."

I finish the martini and place the glass on a ledge and then smile harmlessly at her, and I'm lightly swaying and Blair's looking at the shimmering sea curving toward us and it's miles and miles away.

"I thought of ignoring you but then decided not to," she says, moving closer to me.

"Now I feel pressured but I'm glad you're talking to me." I turn back to the view of the city. "Why didn't you talk to me for so long? What was that about?"

"I was thinking about my own safety."

"Why are you talking to me now?"

"You don't scare me anymore."

"So you've become an optimist."

"I kept thinking I could change you," she says. "All those years."

"But would that have been who you really wanted?" I stop and think it through. "Or would that have been who I really wanted to be?"

"What you really want to be doesn't exist, Clay."

"Why are you laughing when you say that?"

"I wanted to know if you'd talked to Julian," she asks. "Or did you do what I asked you to and just leave it alone?"

"You mean follow your instructions?"

"If you want to put it that way."

"Yeah, I saw him a couple of times and now I guess he's left town for a little while." I pause, then go for it: "Rain told me she doesn't know where he is."

At the mention of her name, Blair says, "You all have a very interesting relationship."

"It's just complicated," I offer casually. "Like it always is."

"She gets around, doesn't she?" Blair asks. "First Julian, then Rip, then Kelly and then you . . ." She pauses. "I wonder who's next."

I don't say anything.

"I'm not judging." She moves closer to me. "But Rain knows where Julian is. I mean, if I know where Julian is, then of course she knows."

"What is the source of your information?" I stop. "Oh, right. Your husband reps her."

"Not really. There's really nothing to rep." She pauses. "I think you know this, too."

"So where is Julian?" I ask.

"Why do you want to know where he is?" she asks. "Are you still friends?"

"Well, we used to be friends," I say. "But, I guess . . . well, no, now we're not. It happens." I pause, then I can't help it. I ask again, "Where is he? How do you know where he is?"

"Just stay out of it," Blair answers softly. "All you need to do is stay out of it."

"Why?"

"Because you'll only make it worse."

I let her kiss me on the lips but there are statues watching us, and lights from the fountains, and behind us the moon is reflected in the horizon of the sea.

"I hear stories about you," Blair says. "I don't want to believe them."

I open the door to the apartment. The lights are off and there's a white rectangle floating low above the couch: a phone glowing in the darkness, illuminating Rip's face. Too drunk to panic I reach for the wall and the room slowly fills with a dim light. Rip waits for me to say something, lounging on the couch as if this is where he's always belonged, an open bottle of tequila in the background. Finally he mentions something about an awards show he was at and, almost as an afterthought, asks me where I've been.

"What are you doing here?" I ask. "How did you get in?"

"I have some friends in the building," Rip says, explaining something supposedly very simple. "Let's take a ride."

"Why?"

"Because your apartment probably isn't"—he squints up at me—"secure."

In the limousine Rip shows me e-mails that were received at Rain's allamericangirlUSA account. There are four of them and I read each one of them on Rip's iPhone in the limo as we cruise along a deserted Mulholland, an old Warren Zevon song hovering in the air-conditioned darkness. At first I'm not even sure what I'm looking at but in the third e-mail I've supposedly written that I *will kill that fucker*—a reference to Rain's "boyfriend" Julian—and the e-mails become maps that need to be redesigned in order to be properly followed, but they're accurate on certain points and have a secret and purposeful strategy to them, though other details about Rain and me don't track, things that have nothing to do with us: the references to kabbalah, comments about a musical number on a recent awards show that I've never seen, Hugh Jackman singing an ironic version of "On the Sunny Side of the Street," my interest in the signs of the zodiac—all of them mistakes in the specifics of our relationship. I keep rereading this e-mail and wondering who wrote these things—clues that are supposed to be followed, an idea that is supposed to lead somewhere—until I realize: It doesn't matter, everything leads to me, I called this upon myself.

"Read the next one, please." Rip reaches over and skips to the next e-mail as casually as if he's flipping through a brochure. "Interesting reference about you and the missing bitch roommate."

In the fourth e-mail I supposedly wrote *and I'll do to Julian what I've already done to Amanda Flew.*

"How did you get these?" I ask, my hands clasped around the iPhone.

"Please" is all Rip says.

"I didn't write these, Rip."

"Maybe you did," Rip says. "Maybe you didn't." He pauses. "Maybe she did. But it's been verified that they were all sent from one of your e-mail accounts."

I keep skimming from one e-mail and then back to another.

"I'll kill that fucker," Rip murmurs. "Doesn't sound

like you, but who knows? . . . I mean, you can be a cold dude sometimes, but . . . these are actually rather heartfelt and sad." He reads from one of them: *"But this time there was an explosion and my feelings as a man cannot be adjusted . . ."* He starts laughing.

"Why are you showing these to me?" I ask. "I didn't write them."

"Because they could potentially incriminate you."

I back away from Rip, unable to mask my loathing. "What movie do you think you're in?"

"Maybe one of the crappy ones you've written," Rip says, not laughing anymore. "Well, then, who wrote them, Clay?" he asks in a forced and playful voice as if he already knew the answer.

"Maybe she wrote them to herself," I mutter in the darkness.

"Or maybe . . . somebody else wrote them," Rip says. "Maybe somebody who doesn't like you?"

I don't say anything.

"Barry warned you about her, huh?" Rip asks.

"Barry?" I murmur, staring into the iPhone. "What?"

"Woolf," Rip says. "Your life coach." He pauses. "The one on Sawtelle." He turns to me. "He warned you about her." He pauses again. "And you didn't listen."

"What if I told you I don't care one way or another?"

"Well, then I'd be very worried for you."

"I didn't write these things."

Rip's not listening. "Haven't you gotten enough out of her?"

"How did you get these, anyway?"

"I mean, I feel for your . . . predicament," Rip says, ignoring the question. "I mean, I really do."

"What's my predicament, Rip?"

"You're too smart to get too involved," Rip says slowly, figuring things out for himself, "so there must be something else that gets you off . . . You're not stupid enough to fall for these cunts, and yet your pain is real . . . I mean everybody knows that you really lost it over Meghan Reynolds . . . That's not a secret, by the way." Rip grins and then his voice grows questioning. "But there's something that's not tracking . . . You're getting off and yet what's the problem?" He turns to me again in the darkness as the limo glides onto Beverly Glen. "Could it be that you actually get off on the fact that because of how you've set things up they'll never love you back? And could it be that"—he pauses, thinking this through—"that you're so much crazier than any of us ever really knew?"

"Yeah, that's it, Rip." I sigh, but I'm shaking. "That's probably it."

"Someone doesn't like you back and never will," Rip says. "At least not in the way you want them to and yet you can still momentarily control them because of the things they want from you. It's quite a system you've set up and maintained." He pauses. "Romance." He sighs. "Interesting."

I keep staring at the iPhone even though I don't want to anymore.

"I guess the consolation is that she's not going to be beautiful forever," he says. "But I'd like to be with her before that happens."

"What are you saying?" I'm asking, the fear pushing forward. "What does any of this mean?"

"It means so many things, Clay."

"I want to get out of here," I say. "I want you to drop me off."

Rip says, "It means she'll never love you." A pause. "It means that everything's an illusion." And then Rip touches my arm. "She's setting you up, *cabron.*"

I offer the phone back to Rip.

"I told you already I don't view you as a threat," Rip says. "You can keep doing whatever you want with her. I don't care because you're not really in the way." He considers something. "Not yet."

Rip takes the phone from me and pockets it.

"But Julian . . . she likes him." Rip pauses. "She's just using you. Maybe that's what gets you off. I don't know. Will she get what she wants? Probably not. I don't know. I don't care. But Julian? For some reason that I can't fathom she *really* likes him. All you're doing is prolonging the situation. You're keeping this in play and she's following your lead because she thinks she's going to be in your movie. And because of this it's moving her closer to Julian." He pauses again. "You don't even realize how afraid you should be, do you?"

Before he drops me off Rip says, "Julian's disappeared." The limousine idles in the driveway of the Doheny Plaza. On the way down Beverly Glen and all across Sunset, Rip texted people back while "The Boys of Summer" kept repeating itself on the stereo. "He's not at his place in Westwood. We don't know where he is."

"Maybe he went to find Amanda," I say, staring out the tinted window at the empty valet stand.

"Shouldn't that be Rain's job?" Rip asks, unfazed. "Oh, I forgot. She has an audition this week, doesn't she?"

"Yes," I say. "She does."

"She doesn't seem very worried about her roommate," Rip says. "At least not as much as being in your little movie."

"How worried should she be, Rip?" I ask. "Where's Amanda?" And then I breathe in before asking, "Do you know?" I stop again. "I mean, you were with her, too. After Rain left you for Kelly? I guess that's when it happened."

"Women aren't very bright," Rip says. "Studies have been done."

I can't see his face. I can only hear his voice, which is, I realize, how I want it.

"What was that about?" I ask. "Revenge? You thought Rain would care that you were fucking her roommate?"

"He's hiding," Rip says, ignoring me.

"Jesus, why don't you let it go?"

"He's hiding." Rip pauses. "I thought maybe you'd know where he is. I thought maybe you'd tell me."

"I don't give a shit where he is."

"Why don't you ask around and then get back to me?"

"Who do you think would know this?" I ask. "Why don't you just talk to Rain?"

He sighs.

"Did you have him beaten up?" I ask. "Was that just a taste of what happens next if he doesn't leave her?"

"You have no imagination," Rip says. "You're actually very by-the-numbers."

Rip leans over and pushes a disc into the CD player.

He sits back. Panting sounds, the wind and the sounds of sex, someone whispering as he has an orgasm, and then it's my voice and I suddenly connect images to the sounds: the bedroom in 1508 in the building looming above us, the view from the balcony, the ghost of a dead boy wandering lost through the space. And then Rain's voice joins mine over the speakers in the back of the limo.

"Turn it off," I whisper. "Just turn it off."

"There's nothing of any use," Rip says, leaning over, ejecting the disc. "That's it."

"Where did you get that?"

"Oh, the common questions you ask."

"I'm not involved with any of this."

"Who knows why people do the things they do?" Rip leans back against the seat, not listening to me. "I can't explain Julian. I don't know why he does the things he does."

I reach for the door handle.

"You discover new things as you go along," Rip says. "You discover things about yourself that you never thought were possible."

I turn back to him. "Why don't you just move on? Let him have her and just move on?"

"I can't do that," he says. "No. I just can't do that."

"Why can't you do that?"

"Because he's compromising the structure of things," Rip says, enunciating each word. "And it's affecting my life."

I'm about to get out of the limousine.

"Don't worry. I won't come around anymore," Rip says. "I'm through with you. It'll play out like it's supposed to play out."

"What does that mean?"

"It means I just wanted to warn you," he says. "You've been officially implicated."

"Don't make contact with me ever—"

"I think you want him gone as much as I do," Rip says before I slam the door shut.

Later that night I dream of the boy again—the worried smile, the eyes wet with tears, the pretty face that looks almost plastic, the photo of Blair and me from 1984 he clutches in one hand, the kitchen knife he's holding in the other as he's floating in the hallway outside the bedroom door, "China Girl" echoing throughout the condo—and then I can't help myself: I rise up from the bed, and I open the door, and I move toward the boy, and when I hit him, the knife falls to the floor. And when I wake up the next morning there's a bruise on my hand from when I hit the boy in my dream.

Rain arrives wearing sweats and no makeup and she's trying to keep it together with the audition set for tomorrow and she didn't want to come over but I told her I would cancel it if she didn't and she's been fasting so we don't go out to dinner and when I first touch her she says let's wait and then I make another threat and the panic is cooled only by breaking the seal off a bottle of Patrón and then I just keep fucking her on the floor in the office, in the bedroom, the lights burning brightly throughout the condo, the Fray blaring from the stereo, and even though I thought she was numb from the tequila she keeps crying and that makes me harder. "You feel this?" I'm asking her. "You feel this inside you?" I keep asking, the fear vibrating all around her, and it's freezing in 1508 and when I ask her if she's cold she says it doesn't matter. And tonight, for maybe the first time, I'm smiling at the black Mercedes that keeps cruising along Elevado, every now and then slowing down so that whoever is behind the tinted windows can look up through the palm trees to the apartment on the fifteenth floor. "I'm just helping you," I tell her soothingly, trying to calm her down, and then she's slurring her words. "Can't you think of anyone but yourself?" she asks. "Why can't you just be chill about this?" she asks when I start touching her again, murmuring how much I love it like this. "Why can't you accept this for what it is?" she asks. She pulls a towel over her body that I just as quickly pull off.

"What is it?" I whisper. I feed her another shot of tequila.

"It's just a movie that you're writing." She's crying openly now as she says this.

"But we're both writing this movie together, baby."

"No we're not," she cries, her face an anguished mask.

"What do you mean?"

"I'm only acting in it."

And when I finally notice the red message light flashing on her cell phone on the nightstand I ask, one hand on her breast, the other one lightly gripping her throat, "Where is he?"

Trent Burroughs calls me and tells me to meet him in Santa Monica after a lunch he's having with a client at Michael's. On the Santa Monica pier Trent's wearing a suit and sitting on a bench at the entrance and when he sees me approaching he looks up from his phone and takes off his sunglasses and just stares at me warily. Trent mentions he finished lunch earlier than he'd planned with a skittish actor he manages, successfully persuading him to take a role in a movie for myriad reasons that would be beneficial to everybody.

"I'm actually surprised you came," Trent says.

"Why couldn't I meet you at the restaurant?" I ask.

"Because I don't really want to be seen with you," he says. "It would validate something that I wouldn't want validated, I guess."

I start walking with him along the boardwalk. He puts his sunglasses back on.

"I suppose I'm more sensitive about things than I thought," he says.

"I got your client an audition today," I say, in a good mood because of how Rain responded to me last night.

"Yeah," Trent says. "You did."

I pause. "Isn't that what you wanted to see me about?"

Trent thinks about it before saying, "In a way."

The empty Ferris wheel looms over us as we pass by barely visible in the haze, just a dim circle, and except for a few Mexican fishermen no one's around. Holiday decorations are still up and a dead Christmas tree wrapped in a garland leans against the peeling wall of the arcade and the faint smell of churros floats toward us from a brightly colored cart and it's hard to concentrate on Trent because the only sounds are the distant surf and the squalling of low-flying gulls, the psychic calling out to us, the calliope playing a Doors song.

"This isn't about Blair?" I suddenly ask.

Trent looks over at me as if he's shocked I would ask that. "No. Not at all. This has nothing to do with Blair."

I keep moving with him down the boardwalk toward the end of the pier, waiting for him to say something.

"I want to make this quick," Trent finally says, checking his watch. "I've got to be back in Beverly Hills by three."

I shrug and put my hands in the pockets of the hoodie I'm wearing, one of them forming a fist around my phone.

"I guess you're going to stop this with Rain Turner, right?" Trent asks. "I mean, the audition's this afternoon, right? And then it'll be over?"

"Stop . . . what, Trent?" I ask innocently.

"Whatever it is you do with these girls." He quickly makes a face, then tries to relax. "This, I don't know, this little game you play."

"What are you talking about, Trent?" I ask, sounding as casual and amused as possible.

"Promise them things, sleep with them, buy them things and then you can only get them so far and when you can't get them the things that you really promised . . ." Trent stops walking and takes off his sunglasses and looks at me, mystified. "Do I really need to say this?"

"It's just a very interesting theory."

Trent stares at me before he continues walking, and then he stops again.

"It's interesting that you—what? Abandon them? Try to screw things up for them once they figure it all out?"

Something in me snaps. "I think Meghan Reynolds is doing okay," I say. "I think she benefited from using me."

"You don't really need to work, do you?" Trent asks. He sounds genuinely interested. "You've got family money, right?"

I don't say anything.

"I mean, you can't afford to live like you do just off screenwriting," Trent says. "I mean, right?"

I shrug. "I do okay." I shrug again.

"I know Rain Turner doesn't have a shot at that role." Trent keeps walking and then he puts his sunglasses back on as if it's the only thing that will calm him down. "I talked to Mark. I talked to Jon. You can keep fucking with her as long as you want, I guess—"

"Trent, you know what? I just realized this is none of your business."

"Well, it has, unfortunately, become my business."

"Really?" I ask, trying to sound neutral. "How's that?"

We're both suddenly distracted by a drunken man in a bathing suit who's gesturing at something invisible in the air at the end of the pier, sunburned, bearded. Trent takes off his sunglasses again and for some reason he doesn't know where to look and he's more agitated than he was before and the land has disappeared behind us and there's no sound coming from the distant shore, which is now completely hidden by haze, and we're out over the water now and two Asian girls pulling tufts of cotton candy off a stick are the only other people wandering by.

"It's much more complicated than you know." Trent says this in a strained voice as he keeps looking around, and I just want him to stop but I also don't want him to look at me. "It's just . . . bigger than you think. All you need to do is, is, is remove yourself," he stammers before regaining his composure. "You don't need to know anything else."

"Remove myself from what, exactly?" I ask. "Remove myself from her?"

Trent pauses a moment, and then decides to tell me something. "Kelly Montrose was a close friend of mine." He lets the statement hang there.

It hangs there long enough for me to ask, "What does Kelly have to do with why I'm here?"

"Rain was with him," Trent says. "I mean, when he disappeared. They were together."

"*With* him?"

"Well, he was paying for it, I guess . . ."

"I thought she had stopped doing that," I say. "I thought she met Rip and that she had stopped doing that."

"She knows things," Trent says. "And so does Julian."

"What things?"

"About what happened to Kelly."

I stare at Trent stone-faced but the fear begins swirling around us softly and it causes me to notice a young blond guy in cargo shorts and a windbreaker leaning against a railing on the pier, purposefully not looking at us, and I realize he could not be more obvious if he were holding a hundred balloons. Invisible gulls keep squalling in the hazy sky above him, and the blond guy suddenly seems familiar but I can't place him.

"I'm not saying she's innocent," Trent's saying. "She's not. But she doesn't need someone like you to make things worse for her."

I turn back to Trent. "But Rip Millar is okay?"

For some reason this question forces Trent to shut up and figure out another tactic.

We start walking again. We pass a Mexican restaurant that overlooks the sea. We're near the end of the pier.

"What did you get out of taking Rain on as a client?" I ask. "I'm curious. Why did you take on a girl you knew was never going to make it?"

Trent keeps matching my steps, and his expression momentarily relaxes. "Well, it made my wife happy to help Julian out before she realized . . ." Trent pauses, thinks things through, and continues. "I mean, I knew about Julian. Blair and I didn't talk about it but it wasn't a secret between us." Trent squints and then puts his sunglasses back on. "If I have any problems they're not with Rain Turner. And they're not with Blair."

"But you have a problem with Julian?"

"Well, I knew that Blair had loaned him a lot of money—well, seventy grand, but for him that's a lot of money." Trent moves alongside me toward the end of the pier, seemingly unaware of the guy who's following us and I keep looking back at. I notice he's holding a camera.

"And I knew she really liked him." Trent pauses. "But I also knew that in the end nothing was going to happen with him."

"And what about me?"

"See, there you go again, Clay," Trent says. "It's not about you."

"Trent—"

"It comes down to this," he continues, cutting me off. "Blair loaned Julian a large sum of money. Julian decided to go to Rip to borrow some cash to pay Blair back. Why? I don't know." Trent pauses. "And that's how Rip met Miss Turner. And, um, the rest is, well, what it is." He pauses again. "Do I need to say anything more? Do you get it?"

I look over at the blond guy again. He's supposed to be in costume, he's supposed to be camouflaged but he's not: it's almost as if he wants us to notice him. He keeps moving down the pier, twenty, maybe thirty yards behind us.

"Rip told me he was going to divorce his wife," I say. "What would they have done then? I mean, if Kelly hadn't shown up? How much longer could they have played this game with Rip if he actually went through with the divorce?"

"No. It was safe," Trent says dismissively. "The divorce would've been too expensive for Rip. They both knew that."

"But then your friend Kelly got in the way," I say.

"That might have been a problem," Trent says, nodding his head.

"The problem being what?"

"Whatever happened between Rip Millar and Kelly

Montrose . . ." Trent stops, figuring out how to phrase it differently. "Kelly knew a lot of people. It's not like Rip Millar was the only person who had issues with him."

My iPhone starts vibrating in the pocket of the hoodie, its sound muffled.

"Actually"—Trent stares at me—"you and Rip have much more in common than you might think."

"Oh, I don't think so," I say. "I didn't have anything to do with Kelly's death."

"Clay—"

"And I don't know how but I think Rip did." I stop walking. "And you knew something at the Christmas party, didn't you? You knew Rip had done something to Kelly. You knew Rain had left him for Kelly and you knew Rip liked her—"

Trent cuts me off. "Yeah? Well, I guess we all have our little theories."

"Theory?" I ask. "It's a *theory* that you knew he was probably dead that night?"

The haze obliterates everything: you can't see the Pacific or the pier behind us, the Mexican restaurant is barely visible at the end of the pier and nothing else at all. The pier falls away into the sea and beyond that is just a sheet of haze blocking out the entire sky so there's no horizon and Trent leans against the railing studying me, still intent on pitching the narrative he wants me to respond to, but I can barely pay attention.

"Why do you keep looking at that restaurant?" Trent suddenly asks. "You thirsty for a margarita or something?"

Trent doesn't realize I'm not looking at the restaurant. The young blond guy in the windbreaker is somewhere around us but I can't see him.

"Why is Kelly Montrose dead?" I say, almost murmuring to myself instead of directing this at Trent. "What happened to Amanda Flew?"

Trent isn't cool enough to hide the desperation that quickly flashes across his face. "It's not just about Kelly and it's not just about Amanda." Trent breathes in and looks around. "You don't understand . . . This . . . thing . . . it has . . . a scope, Clay . . ." Trent stops. "It has a *scope* . . . There are other people involved and it's—"

"Can't you just answer my question?"

"But you're asking for an answer where there isn't just one."

The iPhone in my pocket starts vibrating again.

"You smell like alcohol," he mutters, turning away. "I heard rumors but Christ."

I clasp my fist around the iPhone as if that will make it stop.

"Look, she's not going to get that part," Trent says. "Okay? You understand?"

"Do you know that for sure?"

"Anything could happen, I suppose," Trent says. "But I don't think that's one of them."

"Well, then she won't get the part and then it'll be over," I say. "And then she'll go off with someone else. She'll move on."

"No she won't. Because you'll offer her another one,"

Trent says quickly. "You'll just prolong it. Like you usually do. And like the others, it'll take her a while to understand." Trent stops. "And then, as usual, it'll take even longer for you to understand and—"

"Why are you here, Trent?" I ask, unable to contain the stress that's whispering around us. "What? You're here on Julian's behalf? You want Rain to be with Julian? You want them to live happily ever after?"

"No, no, you're not paying attention. You don't get it," Trent says, shaking his head. "Just stop all contact with her. Starting this afternoon. Don't see her anymore. Don't return her calls. She'll come back to you but don't let her—"

"What if I say go fuck yourself?"

"That would be very stupid."

"Unless you tell me why I should stay away, I don't think what you want is going to happen."

Trent stares at me, and then he tells me something that I know he doesn't want to.

"If she can make Rip Millar happy for a couple more months then everything will calm down." Trent stops and looks into my face. "Do you get it, now? Do I need to explain this any further? Julian's really not the obstacle right now. You are. Julian's already tried to talk her out of being with you. But, in this case, you're the only one she's going to listen to."

"Why me?"

"Because she thinks you're the only one who can do something for her," Trent says, and then shakes his head again. "You're the only one who cares enough." He pauses. "Because she thinks that you're her only chance."

I force myself to laugh but it's just a gesture to overcome the fear. When I reach into my pocket for the iPhone three consecutive texts read: *why are u with him? Why Are You With Him??? WHY ARE YOU WITH HIM???*

I'm not listening to anything Trent says until I hear "As of now, you've officially made yourself a target" because this reminds me of what Rip Millar told me in the back of the limousine a few nights ago. "What?" I look up from the phone and then glance fearfully down the boardwalk at the guy in the windbreaker, who has appeared again, pretending to stare dreamily into the hazy distance.

"Someone could be setting you up," Trent says.

"Being set up for what?"

Trent notices something as I light a cigarette.

"Your hand is shaking," he says. "You can't smoke here."

"I don't think anyone's around to enforce that."

On the roof of the Mexican restaurant someone is scanning the pier with a pair of binoculars. And then I realize that the guy who's been following us is taking more pictures, his camera aimed at the ocean even though the haze makes these pictures almost impossible, unless instead he's taking pictures of two guys leaning against the railing at the end of the Santa Monica pier, one of them smoking a cigarette, the other one backed away from him in frustration. The windbreaker guy crosses the pier again as if he's looking for a better angle and I don't say anything to Trent because he hasn't noticed the guy and the empty roller-coaster cars glide slowly down their tracks, slipping in and out of the haze, and someone faintly sings *you're still the one* from a radio inside a surf shop and on the beach a surfer shuffles through the sand near the water's edge, a towel wrapped around his head like a turban.

"You know she came on to Mark," Trent says. "Or did you know that?"

I keep looking at the phone.

WHAT IS HE TELLING YOU?!?

"She tried to fuck him," Trent says. "He wasn't interested. He laughed about it. It was the night after the audition and she sent him pictures of herself. She told him he could fuck her if he wanted to."

I look back at the roof of the restaurant and then I squint at the blond guy with the camera, now disappearing into the haze.

"He said she was too old for him—"

"Are you trying to make me angry?"

Trent moves into another tactic. "Daniel Carter's interested in doing *Adrenaline*. He wants to make it his next movie. We could make that happen." Trent looks at me hopefully. "Would that *mollify* you?"

"What are you doing, Trent? Why are you here?" I mutter. "If you're not going to talk straight to me then I'm leaving."

"Just walk away. Just leave her alone. I'm just asking you to walk away from her and leave it alone." Trent pauses. "You don't need to know why. You're not going to get any answers. I doubt it would matter to you if you had them anyway."

"I don't give a shit about what you want." I pause. "What I want to know is what happens if I go to the police? What if I lay out a scenario and I think it's a pretty goddamn plausible one about Rip Millar and what happened to Kelly Montrose and what if I go to the police and—"

"No, you won't do that," Trent says tiredly, turning away from me. "You won't do that, Clay."

"Why are you so sure about that?" I toss the cigarette, half smoked, onto the pier and grind it out with my shoe.

"That girl you beat up?" Trent says. "The actress. The one from Pasadena?"

I immediately start walking away from Trent.

"The one that your scumbag lawyer paid off? Two years ago?"

Trent keeps following me.

"She's willing to talk," Trent says, keeping up. "Did you know she was pregnant at the time of the assault? Did you know that she lost the baby?"

Amanda Flew's body is never found but a video of what appears to be her last hours is posted on the Net in a clip and you have to pretend you're not watching it in order to get through it. Amanda is in a motel room nude and incoherent and being shot up by men wearing ski masks. She has a seizure and two of the enormous men hold her down while her body thrashes on the newspapers taped to the floor, and then tools are removed from what looks like a beer cooler. The men take turns urinating on her and they keep slapping her face to keep her awake. And then the seizures become more intense and during one of them an eyeball is dislodged, bulging from its socket, and then a semierect cock is pushed in and out of her slack mouth, and then it's removed once blood starts running down her face, and it's at about this point in the roughly ten minutes of footage that you finally see it: when the drugs start wearing off and Amanda realizes what's going to happen to her and she stares into the camera lucidly for one long moment, her panicked expression becoming something else. And then the thing that makes me shut it off happens: you realize this isn't just about Amanda. I can't help thinking that it's happening because of me.

I avoid everything. Everything goes quiet once the video is posted and yet no one concedes that the video is real. There are actual arguments about its authenticity. People think these are outtakes from a horror movie Amanda shot the year before and not even the makers of the horror movie can stop this new narrative from taking shape. I order two bottles of gin from Gil Turner's and once they're delivered I make plans to leave for Vegas and reserve a suite at the Mandalay Bay but then cancel it even though I've already packed two bags, and the moon rises over the city and for the first time in what seems like years there are no cars on Elevado Street tonight, and in a warm bath I think about calling a girl who I know would come over but then I'm just lying in bed with the Bose headphones, drinking from the second bottle of gin, and then I'm dreaming about the dead boy again and now he's standing in the bedroom, moving softly toward the bed, whispering for me to come join him in his endless sleep, and in the dream the palm trees are taller and bending in the wind outside the sliding glass wall of

1508 and when I see the bruises on his face from where
I struck the boy in the previous dream the phone starts
ringing, waking me up, but not before the boy whispers
Save me . . .

Whut did Rip tell you?"

It's Julian and I'm just waking up and it's late afternoon, the sky dimming into dusk. "What?" I clear my
throat, and ask it again. "What?"

"I know you saw him," he says. "I know he's looking
for me. What did he want?"

I barely manage to sit up. "I think . . . in terms of . . .
what's going on—"

Julian stops me automatically. "There's nothing that's
going to connect him to that." The following silence con-
firms that we both know what he's referencing: Amanda.

"What are you doing?" I ask. "Where are you?"

"We're leaving tonight," Julian says, downplaying the
urgency in his voice.

"Who's leaving?"

"Me and Rain," Julian says. "We're leaving tonight."

"Julian," I start and then try and figure out what I
want to say to him but I'm on the verge of tears and nothing
comes out and I keep clutching the sheets bundled around
me and they're damp with sweat and for the first time it's
real: she's actually leaving with him and not me.

"What?" he asks impatiently. "What is it?"

"I need to see you," I say. "Come over. I want to help
you."

"What?" he asks, annoyed. "Why? Help me with what?"

"Rip wants to make a deal," I say. "He wants this whole thing over with."

There's a pause. "And what do you have to do with this?"

"I know everything," I say. "I'm going to make it happen." I pause before saying, "I'll pay him back." Finally, though I can barely swallow I say, "I'm going to make this end."

Julian sends a text two hours later from somewhere close to the Doheny Plaza. *Are you alone?* And then: *Is it safe to come over?* I've sobered up as much as I can when I text back: *Yes.* When I call Rain there's no answer and because Rain doesn't pick up I dial another number and Rip takes my call.

Someone's been following me," Julian says, brushing past me into the condo. "I took a cab. I'm going to need a ride. You're going to have to drive me back to Westwood." He turns and notices that I'm wearing a robe. He notices the glass of gin I'm holding. He looks at me. "Are you okay? Are you capable of that?"

"Where's Rain?" I ask. "I mean, how is she?"

"Don't bother." Julian walks to the window wall and looks down, craning his neck as if scanning for someone.

"I hear, um, the audition went well—"

"Stop it," he says, turning around.

"She has a shot at the part—"

"It's over, Clay," he says. "That's over. Just don't."

"That's not true, Julian. Hey—"

"I want to know why you've been hanging out with Rip."

"He, um, wants to talk to you," I say. "He just wants to talk to you now that I've agreed to pay him—"

"No, he doesn't," Julian cuts me off.

"Yeah, he really does . . . now that . . ." I'm trying not to stammer. "Don't you get it? I'm paying him back."

Julian's stance changes: he takes a step toward me, then stops. "How did you know about that?" he says. "The money, I mean. Who told you?"

"Trent did," I say. "It was Trent."

"Fuck." Julian turns away again and starts pacing the length of the living room.

I try to come up with something else.

"Hey, I just talked to Rip," I say. "And he said it was cool and . . . I think he just wants to talk."

"He wants Rain," Julian says. "That's what he really wants. And that's not going to happen."

"He gets it," I say. "He just wants to talk to you about . . . something. He just wants to, I don't know, clear things up." I'm struggling to keep my voice steady. "He wants reassurance . . ." I clear my throat and then calmly say: "He thinks you know something that connects him to Kelly."

Julian stares at me and says after a beat, "That's not true."

"He knows that people think he wanted Kelly out of the way," I'm saying.

"That's just a dumb rumor," Julian says, but his voice has changed and something in the room shifts. "Rip doesn't really give a fuck about me."

"Julian," I say, slowly moving toward him, "he had you beaten up."

"How do you know that?"

I swallow. "Because Rip told me."

"Bullshit."

"Yeah, Julian," I say, nodding as I move closer to him. "It was Rip. Rip did that to you . . ."

"No he didn't." Julian waves me off. "That was something else. That wasn't Rip. You're making that up."

"Look," I say, "all I know is that part of the condition on taking the money is that he wants to see you. Tonight. Before you guys leave." I pause. "Otherwise there's no deal."

"Why the fuck does he want to see me when I know he's pissed off? Why doesn't he just take the money?" Julian asks this almost pleadingly. "Don't you think I should probably stay the fuck away from him? Jesus, Clay."

"Because once I told him I'd pay him back—" I start.

"Why are you doing this?" Julian looks at me and then almost automatically realizes why.

"Yeah," I say. "I'd do it for her," I say softly, pulling out my iPhone, and then trying to calm him down: "What's he going to do to you? I'll be there. I'll be with you."

I find Rip's contact info and send him a blank e-mail.

Julian looks at me. He's changing his mind about

something. "You've become friends with him? A month ago you told me he was a freak."

The only thing I can do is counter with: "Why did you go to Rip when you needed the money to pay back Blair?"

"I didn't go to Rip," Julian says. "Rip came to me. Because of Rain he came to me and offered to help me out in exchange for . . ." Julian pauses. "I was trying to figure out another way to pay back Blair, but when Rip came to me it just seemed easier . . . But I didn't go to Rip. He came to me. I didn't go to him."

"Wait, Julian. Hold on."

"What are you doing?"

I'm looking at the response I just received. *Is he with you now?*

I text back: *Give me the address.*

I wait, pretending to read something on the screen.

"Clay," Julian asks, walking toward me. "What are you doing?"

And then: *You'll bring him here?*

An address in Los Feliz appears on the screen barely a second after I text back: *yes.*

Julian calls Rain and I only hear his side of the conversation. It lasts a minute as he tries to calm her down. "We don't know it was him," Julian says. "Hey, chill out . . . We don't know if he took the money." He pauses while pacing the room. "Clay said—" and then he has to stop. "Calm down," he says, almost stunned by the ferocity of the voice coming over the phone. "If you're so worried then confirm it with Rip," he says softly. "Make sure it's happening." Finally Julian looks over at me and says, "No, you don't need to talk to him" and that's my cue to nod. "He's helping us out," Julian says. Once Julian hangs up, my phone immediately starts vibrating in the pocket of the robe I'm wearing and it's Rain and I ignore it.

Julian stands in the bedroom doorway, drinking a bottle of water, watching as I get dressed. I'm pulling on jeans, a T-shirt, a black hoodie. I'm debating whether to give him another chance.

"Rip loaned you the money to pay Blair back?" I ask. "And then what happened?"

"He only loaned part of it," Julian says. "But this has nothing to do with the money. Rip's just using that as an excuse. It's not about the money." He sounds almost scornful.

"You lied to me when you told me you hadn't talked to Blair," I say. "You lied when you said you hadn't talked to her since June and I believed you."

"I know. It was awkward. I felt bad about that. I'm sorry."

I move to the bathroom. I try to brush my hair. My hand is shaking so hard I can't hold the brush.

"I didn't mean to fuck with you," he says.

"I just want to know one thing," I say. "It keeps bothering me."

"What is it?"

"Why did you set me up with Rain if—"

Julian cuts me off as if he knows the rest of the question. "You've been around a long time. You know how this town works. You've been through it before." And then his voice softens. "I just didn't know how fucked up you got over Meghan Reynolds until it was too late."

"Yeah, yeah, yeah, I know that but what I can't understand is that if you knew Rip was so crazy about Rain why did you . . ." I stand in front of Julian, my arms at my sides, but I can't look at him until I force myself to. "Why did you put me in danger?" I ask. "You pushed her onto me even after you knew how Rip felt? You pushed her onto me even though you thought he maybe had something to do with Kelly?"

"Clay, I never thought that he had anything to do with Kelly," Julian says. "Those were just rumors that—"

"You wanted me to help her and I tried, Julian, but now I realize you didn't care whether I got hurt or not."

This moves something in Julian and his face tightens and his voice begins to rise. "Look, it's really cool you're trying to help me out here, but why do you keep thinking Rip was involved with Kelly's death? Do you know something? Do you have any proof? Or are you just making shit up like you always do?"

"What are you talking about?"

"Stop it," he says and suddenly he's a different person. "You've done this so many times before, Clay. I mean, come on, dude, it's a joke. Yeah, you tell people shit, but have you ever really gotten anybody anything?" he asks sincerely. "I mean, you promise shit and maybe you get them closer but, dude, you're lying all the time—"

"Julian, come on, don't—"

"And what I found out is that you really won't do anything for anybody," he says. "Except for yourself." The gentle way he says this forces me to finally turn away. "This, like, delusional fantasy you have of yourself is . . ." He pauses. "Come on, dude, it's a joke." He pauses again. "It's kind of embarrassing."

I force myself to grin in order to lighten the moment and not scare him away.

"Why are you smiling?" he asks.

"It must be a pretty good act," I say. "This . . . fantasy I have of myself."

"Why do you say that?"

"Because you bought into it," I say.

"I never thought you'd actually fall for her."

"Why did you think that?"

"Because Blair told me how cold you could be."

Can you drive?" Julian asks as the elevator heads down to the garage. "Or do you want me to?"

"No, I can drive," I say. "Are you sure you want to do this?"

"Yeah, I'm sure," Julian says. "Let's just get this over with."

"Let him have her," I whisper.

"We're leaving tonight," he says.

"Where are you going?"

"I'm not telling you."

Driving along Sunset I keep checking the rearview mirror and Julian sits in the passenger seat texting someone, probably Rain, and I keep turning on the radio and then turning it off but he doesn't notice, and then we're crossing Highland and the Eurythmics song fades into a voice from the radio talking about the aftershocks from an earthquake earlier, something that I slept through, and I have to roll down all the windows and pull the car over three times in order to steady myself because I keep hearing sirens all around us and my eyes are fixed on the rearview mirror because two black Escalades are following us and the last time I pull over, in front of the Cinerama Dome, Julian finally asks, "What's wrong? Why do you keep stopping?" and where Sunset Boulevard and Hollywood intersect I smile at him coolly as if this is all going to be okay, because in the condo I felt like I was sinking into a rage but now, turning onto Hillhurst, I'm feeling better.

Outside a building past Franklin that's surrounded by eucalyptus trees Julian gets out of the BMW, and starts walking toward the entrance just as I receive a text that says *don't get out of the car,* and when Julian realizes I'm still sitting in the driver's seat he turns around and our eyes lock. A black Escalade pulls up behind the BMW and flashes its headlights over us. Julian leans into the opened passenger window.

"Aren't you coming in?" Julian asks, and then he's squinting at the headlights through the back windshield before they go dark and then he looks at me and I'm just staring blankly at him.

Behind Julian three young Mexican guys are climbing out of the car into the circle of light from a lamppost.

Julian notices them, only mildly annoyed, and then turns back to me.

"Clay?"

"Go fuck yourself."

The moment I say this Julian grabs the door I've already locked and for one moment he leans far enough into the car so that he's close enough to touch my face, but the men pull him back and then he disappears so quickly it's as if he was never here at all.

O n Fountain my phone rings and I pull over somewhere after passing Highland. When I answer the phone I notice that my seat is soaked with urine and it's a call from a blocked number, but I know who it is.

"Did anybody see you bring him here?" Rip asks.

"Rip—"

"No one saw you, right?" Rip asks. "No one saw you bring him here, right?"

"Where am I, Rip?"

The silence is a grin. The silence seals something.

"Good. You can go now."

Rain falls into my arms screaming.

"You drove him there," she screams. "You drove him there?"

I push her against a wall and kick the door closed with my foot.

"Why do you hate me so much?" she screams.

"Rain, sshhh, it's okay—"

"What are you doing?" she screams before I muffle her face with my hand.

And then I push her to the floor and pull off her jeans.

You missed so many hints about me," I whisper to her as she lies drugged in the bedroom.

"I didn't . . . miss them," she says, her face bruising, her lips wet with tequila.

"It's what this place has done to you," I whisper, brushing her hair off her forehead. "It's okay . . . I understand . . ."

"This place didn't do anything to me." She covers her face with her hands, a useless gesture.

She starts crying again, and this time she can't stop.

"Are you going to be sick again, baby?" I hold a damp washcloth against her tan skin as she slips in and out of consciousness. I watch as her hand slowly balls into a fist. I grab her wrist before she can strike me. I push it back down until it relaxes. "Don't hit me again," I say. "It won't matter because I'll just hit you right back," I say. "Do you want that?" I ask.

She shuts her eyes tightly and shakes her head back and forth, tears pouring down her face.

"You tried to hurt me," I say, stroking her face.

"You did that to yourself," she moans.

"I want to be with you," I'm saying.

"That's never going to happen," she says, turning her face away from me.

"Please stop crying."

"That was never going to be part of it."

"Why not?" I ask. I press two fingers on both sides of her mouth and force her lips into a smile.

"Because you're just the writer."

I went to Palm Springs as if nothing had happened. On Highway 111 in the cold desert a massive rainbow appeared, its arc intact, shimmering in the afternoon sky. The girl and boy I bought were in their late teens and the negotiations had gone smoothly and an offer was made and then accepted. The girl and boy were distant. In order to do the things I had paid for they had already checked out before they arrived for the weekend. The girl was impossibly beautiful—the Bible Belt, Memphis—and the boy was from Australia and had modeled for Abercrombie & Fitch and they had come to L.A. to make it but it wasn't happening for them yet. They admitted using fake names. I told them to express themselves only in gestures—I didn't want to hear their voices. I told them to walk around naked and I didn't care how absurd or deranged I seemed. The desert was freezing beneath the dark mountains looming over the town and the palm trees lining the street around the house caged the white sky. I watched geckos dart through the rock garden while the girl and boy sat naked in front of the giant flat-screen TV in the living room watching a remake of *The Hills Have Eyes*.

The ranch house was in the movie colony and had walls that were cream-colored and mirrored and pillars that lined the pool shaped like a baby-grand piano and raked gravel blanketed the yard and small planes flew above it in the dry air before landing at the airport nearby. At night the moon would hang over the silver-rimmed desert and the streets were empty and the girl and the boy would get stoned by the fire pit and sometimes dogs could be heard barking over the wind thrashing the palm trees as I pounded into the girl and the house was infested with crickets and the boy's mouth was warm but I didn't really feel anything until I hit him, always panting, my eyes gazing at the steam rising from the pool at dawn.

Complaints had been made because the girl had become frightened of "the situation." The manager of the girl and the boy wanted to speak to me at one point and I renegotiated the price and then handed the cell phone back to the boy and he spoke briefly into it before handing the phone back to me. Everything was confirmed. And then the boy took turns fucking me and then the girl and my fingers kept jamming into him, spurring the boy on, and the human skull in the plastic bag was a prop watching us from the nightstand in the bedroom and sometimes I made the girl kiss the skull and her eyes were in a trance and she gazed at me as if I didn't exist and then I'd tell the boy to beat the girl and I watched as he threw her to the floor and then I told him to do it again.

One night the girl tried to escape from the house and the boy and I chased her down the street with flashlights and then onto another street where he tackled her just before dawn. We dragged the girl quickly back inside the house and she was tied up and put in what I had told them to refer to as the kennel, which was her bedroom. "Say thank you," I told the girl when I brought out a plate of cupcakes laced with laxative and made the girl and boy eat them because it was their reward. Smeared with shit, I was pushing my fist into the girl and her lips were clinging tightly around my wrist and she seemed to be trying to make sense of me while I stared back at her flatly, my arm sticking out of her, my fist clenching and unclenching in her cunt, and then her mouth opened with shock and she started shrieking until the boy lowered his cock into her mouth, gagging her, and the sound of crickets kept playing over the scene.

The sky looked scoured, remarkable, a cylinder of light formed at the base of the mountains, rising upward. At the end of the weekend the girl admitted to me that she had become a believer as we sat in the shade of the towering hills—"the crossing place" is what the girl called them, and when I asked her what she meant she said, "This is where the devil lives," and she was pointing at the mountains with a trembling hand but she was smiling now as the boy kept diving into the pool and the welts glistened on his tan back from where I had beaten him. The devil was calling out to her but it didn't scare the girl anymore because she wanted to talk to him now, and in the house was a copy of the book that had been written about us over twenty years ago and its neon cover glared from where it rested on the glass coffee table until it was found floating in the pool in the house in the movie colony beneath the towering mountains, water bloated, the sound of crickets everywhere, and then the camera tracks across the desert until we start fading out on the yellowing sky.

When I did a search for the name of the dead boy a link moved me to a Web site he had created before his death called the Doheny Project. A thousand pictures detailed the renovation of unit 1508 in the Doheny Plaza and then abruptly stopped. There were pictures of the boy as well, headshots of him blond and tan and flexing—he had wanted to be an actor—and there was the fake smile, the pleading eyes, the mirage of it all. The boy had posted pictures of himself in the club he was at the night he died, high and shirtless surrounded with boys who looked like him and this was before he went to sleep and never woke up, and in one of the shots I could see that he had the same tattoo that Rain had seen when she dreamed about him—a dragon, blurred, on his wrist. And the search led me to an audition reel and in one of the auditions the boy reads the part of Jim in *Concealed*, the movie I wrote. "What's the worst thing that ever happened to you, Jimmy?" someone playing a girl named Claire reads off camera. "Unconditional love," the boy says, the character of Jimmy turning away in mock shame, but the boy was reading the line wrong, giving it the wrong emphases, smirking when he should have been totally serious, turning it into a punch line when it was never supposed to be a joke.

When Laurie calls from New York I tell her she has a week to move out of the apartment below Union Square. "Why?" she asks. "I'm subletting it," I tell her. "But why?" she asks. "Because I'm staying in L.A.," I tell her. "But I don't understand why," she says again, and then I tell her, "Everything I do is for a reason."

At a fund-raising concert at Disney Hall that has something to do with the environment I talk to Mark during the intermission and where I ask him about Rain Turner's audition for *The Listeners*. Mark tells me that Rain was never going to get the role of Martina but she's actually being considered for a much smaller role as the older sister—basically, one scene where she's topless—and that they're going to see her again next week. We're standing at the bar when I tell him, "Don't, okay? Just don't." Mark looks at me, a little surprised, and then there's a little smile. "Okay, I get it." At the reception afterward at Patina I run into Daniel Carter, who says he's very serious about making *Adrenaline* his next film after he finishes shooting the movie Meghan Reynolds is costarring in. Daniel is also thinking of using Rain Turner in the movie Meghan Reynolds is costarring in—Trent Burroughs made a call, said it would be a favor, whatever, it's three lines. I tell Daniel to do a favor for me and not to put Rain in the movie and that Rain's more trouble than she's worth and Daniel seems shocked but I mistake this for amusement.

"I heard you were with her," Daniel says.

"No," I say. "I wouldn't call it that."

"What happened?" he asks, as if he already knows, as if he's waiting to see if I'll keep it secret.

"She's just a whore," I say, shrugging jovially. "The usual."

"Yeah?" Daniel asks, smiling. "I heard you like whores."

"In fact I'm writing a script about her," I say. "It's called *The Little Slut.*"

Daniel looks at the ground before glancing up at me again, an attempt to hide his embarrassment. I knock back the rest of my drink.

"Anyway, she's with Rip Millar now," Daniel says. "Maybe he'll help her out."

"I don't get it," I say. "How could Rip help her?"

"You didn't know?" Daniel asks.

"Know what?"

"Rip left his wife," Daniel says. "Rip wants to make movies now."

Julian's body is found almost a week after he disappeared, or was kidnapped, depending on which script you want to follow. Earlier that week three young Mexican men connected to a drug cartel were found shot to death in the desert, not far from where Amanda Flew was last seen. They were decapitated and their hands were missing and

they had at one point during the last week been in posses-
sion of a black Audi that was found outside of Palm Desert,
torched.

Someone filmed me with a digital camera in the American Airlines first-class lounge at JFK when I was sitting at a
table with Amanda Flew last December. A disk is mailed to
me in a manila envelope with no return address. The scene
comes back to me: Amanda reading my palm in the Admiral's Club, the empty glasses on the table, both of us laughing suggestively, leaning into each other, and though the
lighting and sound quality are bad and you can't hear what
we're saying it's obvious I'm flirting hard. Sitting in my
office watching this play on the screen of my monitor I realize this is where everything started. Rain picked Amanda up
from LAX in the blue Jeep on that night in December and
then they followed me back to Doheny because Amanda had
told Rain she met the guy Julian had been telling her about.
I heard you met a friend of mine, Rip told me outside the W
Hotel last December at the premiere of Daniel Carter's
movie. *Yeah, I heard you really hit it off . . .* When the
footage ends a series of doctored pictures fade in and out of
one another: Amanda and me holding hands in line at
Pink's, wheeling a cart out of the Trader Joe's in West Hollywood, at Amoeba, standing in the lobby of the ArcLight.
All of the pictures are faked but I get it—this is a warning of
some kind. And right when I'm about to eject the disk Rip
calls me, as if he's timed it, as if he knows what I'm looking

at, and he tells me another video will be arriving soon and that I need to watch that one as well.

"What is it?" I ask. I keep staring at the photos fading in and out: Amanda and me buying star maps on Benedict Canyon, the two of us standing in front of the Capitol Records Building like we were tourists, at an outside table on the patio at the Ivy having lunch.

"Just something somebody sent to me," Rip says. "I think you should see it."

"Why?" I'm staring at a photo of Amanda and me in the black BMW in the parking lot of the In-N-Out in Sherman Oaks.

"It's persuasive," Rip says, and then he tells me that the licenses for the club he wants to open in Hollywood have finally been approved, and that I should stop telling people not to put Rain in their movies.

The new disk arrives that afternoon. I remove the disk of Amanda Flew and me at JFK and put the new disk into the computer but I turn it off almost immediately once I see what it is: Julian tied to a chair, naked.

After I drink enough gin to calm down I stand at my desk in the office. They had drawn lines with a black marker all over his body—the "nonlethal entry wounds" as the Los

Angeles County coroner's office was quoted in the *Los Angeles Times* article about the torture-murder of Julian Wells. These are the stab wounds that will allow Julian to live long enough to understand that he will slowly bleed to death. There are more than a hundred of them drawn all over his chest and torso and legs as well as his back and neck and the head which has been freshly shaved, and when I'm able to look back at the screen one of the hooded figures standing over Julian whispers something to another hooded figure but the second I pause the disk I get a text from a blocked number that asks *What are you waiting for?* About twenty minutes into the disk I mistake static for the clouds of flies swarming around the room below the flickering fluorescent lights and crawling over Julian's abdomen which has been painted dark red, and when Julian starts screaming, weeping for his dead mother, the video goes black. When it resumes Julian's making muffled sounds and that's when I realize they've cut out his tongue and that's why his chin is slathered with blood, and then within a minute he's blinded. In the final moments of the disk the sound track is of the threatening message I left on Julian's phone two weeks ago and accompanied by my drunken voice the hooded figures start punching him randomly with the knives, chunks of flesh spattering the floor, and it seems to go on forever until the cement block is raised over his head.

At the Hollywood Forever Cemetery I recognize very few of the people who show up for the memorial and they're mostly just figures from the past who I don't know anymore and I wasn't even going to go but I had finished two projects in the last couple days that I had been ignoring, one was a remake of *The Man Who Fell to Earth* and the other was a script about the reformation of a young Nazi, and the last scene I wrote was when a boy in a castle is being shown a row of fresh corpses by a madman in a uniform who keeps asking the boy if he knows any of the dead and the boy keeps answering no but he's lying, and I was staring at the bottle of Hendrick's that sat on my desk while on the TV in my office Amanda Flew's mother was being interviewed on CNN, after she had filed a complaint about the release of the video but she was told that privacy rights don't extend to the dead even though Amanda's body hasn't been found, and there was a montage of Amanda's brief career with "Girls on Film" playing on the sound track as the piece segues into the dangers of the drug wars across the border, and I was trying to make a decision that seemed daunting either way and for a moment I thought about checking out.

I arrive late just as the memorial concludes, and I'm standing in the back of the room scanning the small crowd as Julian's father walks by and doesn't recognize me. Rain isn't here and neither is Rip, who for whatever reason I thought would be, and Trent didn't show up but Blair's here with Alana and I duck out before she sees me, and then I'm walking past the Buddhist cemetery where the dead are guarded by mirror-lined stupas and peacocks roam the graves and I'm staring up at the Paramount water tower, through the bristling palm trees, and I'm wearing a Brioni suit that had once fit but is now too loose and I keep thinking I see figures lurking behind the headstones but I tell myself it's just my imagination, taking my sunglasses off, squeezing my eyes shut. The cemetery pushes up to the back walls of the Paramount lot and you could find meaning in that or be neutral about it in the same way you could find something ironic about the endless rows of the dead lined up beneath the palm trees with their fronds blooming against a sparkling blue sky or choose not to, and I'm looking at the sky thinking it's the wrong time of day for a memorial, but the day, the sunlight, chases the ghosts away and isn't that the point? They show movies here during the summer, I remember, studying the giant white wall of the mausoleum where the movies are projected.

"How are you?"

Blair is standing over me. I'm sitting on a bench next to a tree but there's no shade and the sun is burning.

"I'm okay," I say in a hopeful voice.

She doesn't take her sunglasses off. She's wearing a black dress that accentuates her thinness.

From where I'm sitting I watch the dispersing crowd, their cars pulling out onto Santa Monica Boulevard, and farther away there's a bulldozer digging a fresh grave.

"I guess I'm worried," I say. "A little."

"Why?" she asks, sounding concerned, like someone trying to comfort a child. "About what?"

"I've been questioned twice," I say. "I had to hire a new lawyer." I pause. "They think I'm involved."

Blair doesn't say anything.

"They say there were witnesses who saw me with him the night of his disappearance and . . ." I look away from her and don't mention that the only person I could imagine this to be true of now that I'm sure the three Mexicans are dead is the doorman at the Doheny Plaza but when the doorman was interviewed he couldn't remember anything and there were no records because I'd told him before Julian arrived that I was expecting a delivery and to just send up whoever stopped by, and all I've done is deny everything and tell everyone that I might have seen Julian earlier that week but the fact remains I don't have an alibi for the night I drove him to the corner of Finley and Commonwealth and I know Rip Millar and Rain both know this. "Which means . . . well, I don't know what it means," I murmur, and then try to smile. "A lot of things, I guess." The Hollywood sign blares from the hills and a helicopter flies low over the cemetery and a small group dressed in black is wandering through the headstones. I've only been here for fifteen minutes.

"Well," Blair starts haltingly, "if you didn't do anything, why are you worried?"

"They think I might have been part of . . . a plan," I say casually. "I actually heard the word 'conspiracy' used."

"What can they prove?" she asks softly.

"They have a tape someone thinks is incriminating . . . this . . . this drunken rant I made at Julian one night and . . ." I stop. "Well, I was sleeping with his girlfriend so . . ." I look up at her and then away. "I think I know who's involved and I think they're going to get away with it . . . but no one knows where I was."

"Don't worry about that," Blair says.

"Why shouldn't I worry?" I ask.

"Because I'll tell them you were with me."

I look up at her again.

"I'll tell them you were with me that night," she says.

"I'll tell them we spent the entire night together. Trent was away with the girls. I was alone."

"Why would you do that?" This is a question you ask when you don't know what else to say.

"Because . . ." she starts, then stops. "I guess I want something in return." She pauses. "From you."

"Yeah?" I say, squinting up at her, the muffled sounds of traffic on Gower somewhere in the distance behind me.

She holds out a hand. I wait a beat before reaching out to take it but once I stand up I let it go. *She's a witch*, someone whispers into my ear. *Who is she?* I ask. *She's a witch*, the voice says. *Like all of them.*

Blair takes my hand again.

I think I realize what she wants but it's not until I see Blair's car that it finally announces itself clearly. It's a black Mercedes with tinted windows not unlike the one that had followed me across Fountain or the one that cruised by the Doheny Plaza all those nights or the one that tailed the blue Jeep whenever it was parked on Elevado or the one that followed me in the rain to an apartment on Orange Grove. And in the distance the same blond guy I saw at the Santa Monica pier with Trent and at the bar in Dan Tana's and crossing the bridge at the Hotel Bel-Air, and talking to Rain outside Bristol Farms one morning last December is leaning against the hood of the car and stops shading his eyes with his hand when he sees me staring at him. I thought he was maybe looking at the graves but then I realize he's watching us. He turns away when Blair nods at him. I keep staring at the car while I feel Blair's fingers lightly stroking my face. *Just go where she says*, the voice sighs. *But she's a witch*, I whisper back, still staring at the car. *And her hand is a claw . . .*

"Your face," she says.

"What about it?"

"You don't look like anything has happened to you," she whispers. "And you're so pale."

There are many things Blair doesn't get about me, so many things she ultimately overlooked, and things that she would never know, and there would always be a distance between us because there were too many shadows every where. Had she ever made promises to a faithless reflection in the mirror? Had she ever cried because she hated someone so much? Had she ever craved betrayal to the point where she pushed the crudest fantasies into reality, coming up with sequences that only she and nobody else could read, moving the game as you play it? Could she locate the moment she went dead inside? Does she remember the year it took to become that way? The fades, the dissolves, the rewritten scenes, all the things you wipe away—I now want to explain these things to her but I know I never will, the most important one being: I never liked anyone and I'm afraid of people.

1985–2010

ALSO BY BRET EASTON ELLIS

LESS THAN ZERO

Set in Los Angeles in the early 1980s, this cooly mesmerizing novel is a raw, powerful portrait of a lost generation. They have experienced sex, drugs, and disaffection at too early an age, and lived in a world shaped by casual nihilism, passivity, and too much money. Clay comes home for Christmas vacation from his Eastern college and reenters a landscape of limitless privilege and absolute moral entropy, where everyone drives Porches, dines at Spago, and snorts mountains of cocaine. He tries to renew his feelings for his girlfriend, Blair, and for his best friend from high school, Julian, who is careering into hustling and heroin. Clay's holiday turns into a dizzying spiral of desperation that takes him through the seamy world of L.A. after dark.

Fiction/978-0-679-78149-3

THE RULES OF ATTRACTION

Set at a small, affluent liberal-arts college in New England, this novel is about three students with no plans for the future, or even the present, who become entangled in a romantic triangle. Lauren changes boyfriends every time she changes majors and might be writing love letters to hard-drinking Sean, a hopeless romantic, who only has eyes for Lauren, even if he ends up in bed with half the campus and with Paul, Lauren's ex, who is forthrightly bisexual and whose passion masks a shrewd pragmatism. *The Rules of Attraction* is a poignant, hilarious take on the death of romance.

Fiction/978-0-679-78148-6

AMERICAN PSYCHO

American Psycho is set in a world (Manhattan) and an era (the 1980s) recognizably our own. The wealthy elite grows wealthier, the poor are turned out onto the streets in droves, and anything seems possible. Patrick Bateman—the handsome, well-educated, and wealthy young man who works by day on Wall Street and expresses his true self through torture and murder—prefigures an apocalyptic horror that no society could bear to confront.

Fiction/978-0-679-73577-9

THE INFORMERS

Dirk sees his best friend killed in a desert car wreck, then rifles through his pockets for a last joint before the ambulance comes. Cheryl, a wannabe newscaster, chides her future stepdaughter, "You're tan but you don't look happy." Jamie is a clubland carnivore with a taste for human blood. As rendered by Ellis, their interactions compose a chilling, fascinating, and outrageous descent into the abyss beneath L.A.'s pretty surfaces.

Fiction/978-0-679-74324-8

GLAMORAMA

Manhattan in the 1990s: the center of the world or the vortex of some other universe. Victor Ward, a model with perfect abs and all the right friends, is seen and photographed everywhere, even in places he hasn't been and with people he doesn't know. He's living with one beautiful model and having an affair with another on the eve of opening the trendiest nightclub in New York history. And now it's time to move on to the next stage. But the future he gets is not the one he had in mind. *Glamorama* takes us into a shadowy looking-glass world where fame and fashion and terror and mayhem become confused and then begin to resemble the all too familiar surface of our lives.

Fiction/978-0-375-70384-3

Bret Ellis, the narrator of *Lunar Park*, is a writer whose first novel, *Less Than Zero*, catapulted him to international stardom while he was still in college. In the years that followed, he found himself adrift in a world of wealth, drugs, and fame, as well as dealing with the unexpected death of his abusive father. After a decade of decadence, a chance for salvation arrives; the chance to reconnect with an actress he was once involved with, and their son. But almost immediately his new life is threatened by a freak sequence of events and a bizarre series of murders that all seem to connect to Ellis's past. Reality, memoir, and fantasy combine to create not only a fascinating version of this most controversial writer but also a deeply moving novel about love and loss, parents and children, and ultimately, forgiveness.

Fiction/978-0-375-72727-6